For Neal and Stevie.

Thanks to:

Neal, Colleen, Christine, Ruby, Catherine, Robert, Bruce, and Stevie.

"Winter knows the good are poor,
that talent goes begging warmth
from ice and snow."

—From the poem
*Winter Lyric*
by Irving Layton
(1967)

# WINTER LYRIC

*A novella*
Michael Whone

©2018
originally published 2017
978-1-7753300-2-8

# Foreword

The following pages contain words that I have come to know very personally in the past year. It is a narrative of love, loss, loneliness and pain unlike any other I have come across, but those words on their own cheapen it and make me sound like the back cover of a DVD. It is a meditation on all that is gained, and all that is lost, in every small moment, every seemingly meaningless interaction that passes us by, and it is told in a voice that is both profound and inimitable. It was written by my friend and brother-in-arms, Michael Whone, and contains more beauty and pain than should rightly exist in its brief pages.

Elliot's story begins in what seems like a confused static of thoughts and moments, shifting easily between painful past moments and mundane present ones, old shames and missed opportunities, and present painful solitude. When a day breaks for him, though, he finds a clarity, joy and beautiful order to his world that I could not help but be in envy of. Elliot stitches himself together again and again with the pieces of humanity that are presented to him, and revels in the fragile beauty of it all.

I won't be so trite as to label my friend's story a simple tale of unrequited love. Elliot nakedly faces the injustices we all do just by being born into this world, and the painful path a person must take to make a place for themselves in this world, when none is made for them.

—Neal O'Reilly
*Thursday December 1, 2016*

# Chapter One

*Wednesday October 1, 2014*

April looked in December, the month following Monday. September ended minutes ago, and the next time December starts on a Tuesday is next year. The last time that happened was five years ago and eleven years before that December started on a Tuesday as well. I was twenty-six and fifteen, respectively. When I was twenty-six, I started my little blue diary because December started on a Tuesday. When I was fifteen, I had just broken up with my first girlfriend, and now I'm thirty-one. It was different this time with Sarah, but it reminded me of that first time with April.

Nina responded demurely to every advance I ever made toward her. So, I moved on and I had a cigarette. I stole Nina's only cigarette before I left her to move on. She said every time she had a cigarette she thought of everything she ever did wrong. Well, I think she needed to lose that cigarette because I don't think it was immediately apparent to her that what she did wrong was let me move on.

Moving on—

Some people are today, some people are tonight, and some people are tomorrow. Some people do their work well and get to bed and make the world turn around and either complain that they don't get what they deserve or they just appreciate how swimmingly life is turning out. Those people are today. Some people barely make it through the day, making errors every which way, losing every job they've been given, hoping to have an even crazier party tonight, and they end up passing out, or wishing there were more cigarettes in their packs at one o'clock in the morning or they end having blood gushing down their noses and stealing tomorrow's tequila. Those people are tonight. And some people are natural at everything they do in every way and in every effortless attempt they make they are unknowingly rewarded with love and affection and anything tangible that they didn't even know they wanted from life. Those people are tomorrow. You'll know you're looking at tomorrow when you see his red eyes when you're craving that cigarette at a minute past one in the morning.

You should know I found a cigarette. You should know I stole a shot of Shawn's unopened tequila bottle he was saving for his dad's birthday. You should know I waited until Shawn was asleep with red eyes so he didn't pop me one. You should know I thought about everything I did wrong. I crashed a car, that's the real problem. Well, I lost my job, that's the real problem. Well, I haven't loved anyone in a long time, that's the real problem. So that's the past and I've moved on, I swear.

I think if I had a cigarette with me that night I killed a man, colliding with his car, it would have been easier to move on. I probably wouldn't have fallen asleep in the first place but because of the arguments I was having with my parents about the accident, I moved out and met a cute, young black woman. The summer after that, I met April. I met April eight years ago. That was the last time I was romantic with a woman.

I'm perplexed. How do I put the satisfaction of being with Sarah Benton last night in context with the heartbreak-notoriety my life has seemed like? Since being with Sarah romantically last night, I wish I could see Shawn, my one true friend, climb in through his window after midnight like I always used to and talk through the feelings I have had about Sarah and all the other women that are rushing to mind.

I saw Shawn for the last time nine years ago, two days after I was alone with the cute, black woman. I met her after I moved out because of my car accident when I was twenty-two. She came to my room one night and she asked me to play music for her. She requested Billy Holiday so I sang her *God Bless the Child*. I thought she wanted me to kiss her and I would have liked to but really, I wanted her to come to Ottawa with me the next day to meet Shawn.

She didn't come but I went to Ottawa anyway. I left the following night. When I arrived in Ottawa, I went for breakfast with Shawn at the diner across the street from the other diner where we used to practice hitting on women, using the waitresses as test subjects. Needless to say, they didn't like it and it never worked. We had to switch diners I guess because Shawn had a girlfriend that time, nine years ago.

After breakfast, we went into the little Native arts and crafts store right beside the diner and bought a pack of *Natives*. Literally, they were packs of cigarettes from behind the counter that were labeled *Native*. So we went up to his apartment beside the Salvation Army and smoked *Natives*. Shawn's friend Alex came by claiming that if I was around long enough, I'd be able to buy some super cheap *Natives* as part of some deal he was cooking up later in the week. Luckily, I was planning to stay a week. I think that's why the cute woman didn't want to come with me.

Just before I left for Ottawa, and the black woman and I were in my room, my so-called friend, Christian, came to visit me with his cousin. Christian lied to the cops and told them I hadn't slept much, that it caused the car accident. So, I ended up leaving my parents' home over fights we were having about being charged for driving carelessly. Christian also broke up my encounter that night with the black woman. If he hadn't shown up, she would have been the first woman, in a long time, that I became amorous with and I wouldn't have had to wait a year to meet April. The cute woman left when Christian got there. She told me she'd come back later but she didn't and then I took off on the greyhound for Ottawa the next night.

My parents talk about Christian like it was yesterday, even though I haven't seen him since that summer. I haven't seen that cute woman since that summer either but I met April the following summer and to be honest, I haven't had much luck with women since. April took my virginity the day I met her and there's been no women since then. Being sexual with Sarah last night reminded me of all this.

Today I quit smoking and my parents bought me some liquid for my electronic cigarette and then we went for coffee and they kept talking about how Christian ruined my life. It's a common topic because I can't find a job and that particular time in my life is the crux of my failures. There was some good in the bad, and April was that—but Sarah—Sarah isn't the good in the bad.

It's funny that the crux of my failures was named Christian though, because I go to church quite regularly. I'm on the payroll as a member of the worship band in my congregation, and I even go to bible study. It was an attempt to turn my life around. The attempt proved to be fruitful because now that I think about it, I met Sarah the first night I skipped bible study. Well, I met her before it was about to start and we talked for a couple hours and chain smoked and I walked her home and kissed her on the cheek the next time I saw her.

At first, when I saw her, Sarah was wearing the same shirt Nina wore the last time I saw her. It felt like she was starting from where I'd left off with Nina. Those first couple weeks I was reminded of Nina. Nina was the one that broke my heart, and our relationship ended when I realized her intentions weren't the same as mine. I haven't seen her in just over nine years, a couple years after my first two years of college in Toronto. Meeting Sarah was the first stabilizing moment with a woman in the nine years that passed between visiting Shawn in Ottawa and now.

It kind of helped that I didn't think deeply about Nina much longer after meeting Sarah, but she started reminding me of Stephanie. Stephanie was one of the sweetest girls I've ever known. Stephanie was my best friend in high school, the first girl I ever slept beside.

When I was in Ottawa, the last time I saw Shawn, nine years ago, there was a girl there named Irene that looked exactly like Stephanie. One night during the week I spent there, a group of us took a long walk along the river and behind parliament hill with a couple of bottles of wine. It was Irene's last night in Ottawa. She was moving to Montreal. I was completely broke and Irene was going to buy a greyhound ticket to Montreal in the morning.

Coincidentally, for a year, I had kept a Greyhound ticket

from Ottawa to Montreal in my wallet. I had bought a ticket from Toronto to Montreal to visit Nina but when I got to Ottawa I lost my nerve and went back to Toronto instead. The ticket from Ottawa to Montreal still remained. If I had gone to Montreal that time to see Nina, the woman that later broke my heart the night I stared into Shawn's red eyes, I don't know what would have happened, but like I said, I'm moving on. So, I ended up selling that ticket to Irene for ten dollars. I borrowed two dollars from Shawn and bought chicken fingers at the Elgin Street Diner on the way back to Shawn's place. I also urinated on the Lord Elgin hotel.

When we got back to Shawn's place, Shawn and his girlfriend went to bed and I thought that I would write a song for the first time in my life. I borrowed Shawn's roommate's guitar, stayed up during the night and started to write my first song. I wasn't quite sure what to write the lyrics about. The thought of not visiting Nina with that ticket came to mind. I actually did visit her in Montreal once and got drunk in her dorm on Portuguese wine that I bought from the corner store a couple blocks away.

As I was playing, I heard some noises, then all of a sudden there was a guy I'd never seen before in the living room sitting in front of me, asking who I was and what I was doing. Apparently he had climbed through the kitchen window and was expecting Shawn there to talk to him. He was Shawn's friend. I asked him why he came and he said he came because he was melancholy that the girl he had been seeing was moving to Montreal. As he was telling me the story of their last moments together, I was writing down what he was saying and using it as lyrics in my song.

At the break of dawn I received a tax credit and I finished my first song. I went to the gas station across from Shawn's building and bought some junk food and then I went to sleep. In the afternoon, Alex came by and he told me his deal for the cigarettes had fallen through. As a consolation, he offered me some counterfeit bus passes. I played him my song, *Mixing Meta-Flowers*. It was the first time I had ever played that song for anyone. It was a meta song because the last night with your true love is a relatable experience but it wasn't meta specifically regarding me.

It's funny how a song can just come to you in the night, like that guy in Shawn's window, like Sarah last night. I had never written a song before, I was over three-hundred kilometers away from home, I had been playing music professionally for four years and for some reason, it was the night and everything in it that brought the song out of me and made it magic. The song I had written about drinking for the last time with your true love was real magic.

# Chapter Two

*Sunday, October 5, 2014*

It had been twelve years since I kissed a woman. The way things were going, before being amorous with Sarah less than a week ago, I thought I might have had to wait thirteen years to kiss a woman again. Those couple of nights Sarah and I were together, over the past two weeks, were very memorable for me. I'm glad it's only been twelve years because I'd be lucky on one hand that I'd get to kiss a woman again but on the other hand I'd be unlucky if it was thirteen years since the last time. It was Thanksgiving twelve years ago when I kissed that woman at the bar in my hometown. I was living in Toronto and visiting home for Thanksgiving. Victoria had stayed in Toronto for Thanksgiving.

I'm not home right now either. I live here, but I don't think I'll ever consider this city my hometown. I moved here seven years ago, about two hundred kilometers south of my hometown, a hundred kilometers north of Toronto. My sister moved here to further her college education and I followed her here with my parents to get away from the family of the man I killed. They weren't harassing me but I felt I was an unnecessary presence to them so I moved here in silent sympathy.

When I moved here, I didn't meet any women until two years later. Two of them, in fact, and they became the subjects at the beginning of my little blue diary. It didn't work out with either of them. It must have been the greeting committee for my new place of residence. I must have been on the waiting list. Neither of the two stuck around.

For the next five years I didn't become close with any women at all until I met Sarah. Sarah was with me on my birthday, yesterday, which is just before Thanksgiving. Although, I'm not quite sure she was with me as much as she was being tonight by herself. She left me drunk and alone. I was expecting her to stay with me because it was my birthday.

Sarah and I went to the liquor store early yesterday. I bought some rum and a bottle of wine. I told her I wanted to drink something special so I would remember my birthday. She looked beautiful. She was wearing a cardigan sweater, a short black skirt with brand new black leotards and a scarf tied around her neck. She complained that it was cold out. She got herself a bottle of wine, a couple of dark beers and a small bottle of vodka. After we left the liquor store, she told me she'd come over later.

When she came back, she had changed her clothes and she was wearing a black jacket she got for seven dollars at a thrift shop. She was wearing the same leotards, a white shirt and a slightly longer black skirt with white polka dots. We were out on my porch having a cigarette when my friend and neighbour, Eric, came to see us. Sarah asked him to come with us to her friend's party. Without question he came.

Last summer she kissed Eric in front of me. The week before

they kissed, Sarah and I went to a party at his place and I sent him a message on the phone saying that I loved Sarah. He read it out loud as the three of us sat together. Later on that night, Sarah left and went to Eric's room with him for about an hour. It was a late hour and she left after that. When Eric came down, I asked him if I could talk to him privately. We went outside and I asked him what happened and he said he didn't do anything romantic with her. I still don't believe him.

The next weekend we went to another party there and Sarah was ignoring me and by the time it got late she was getting very flirty with Eric. He kissed her as I played Billy Holiday's *What a little Moonlight Can Do* on the stereo and other romantic songs. I thought the Billy Holiday song was fitting because of the lyrics. I couldn't stick around to suffer much longer so I left overwhelmed with jealousy. In the morning, Eric came over and sat on my couch. "All I did," he said "was kiss her, we didn't do anything else."

"I'm surprised," I replied, "I played the most beautiful music for you." I guess it serves me right because I didn't kiss her the first opportunity she gave me. I don't think a lot about Sarah and Eric kissing but that thirteen year estimate was on my mind quite a bit this past week.

When I lived in Toronto for my first two years of college, I used to spend a lot of time with Victoria. She was a poet and studied literature at the University of Toronto. I remember keenly going to buy gloves with her in my first year of college, back when I still studied music. Since then, buying a pair of gloves has always been a fall tradition, except that I've had to do it alone because no women have been in my life much since my first sexual experience with April. I have met women—some of them in my new city, but none of them really became close and stuck around.

Victoria and I went to a movie on my twenty-first birthday, just after the start of my second year of college, eleven years ago. After the movie we were talking. She stopped me and said she was with her ex-boyfriend the previous week. She didn't just kiss him either, she had sex with him at his house. We went back to Victoria's place and she had planned a surprise party for me. Nina came. I really hate surprise parties. I imagine it's what it feels like to have sex with a prostitute. You're excited at the idea but you can't get fully aroused because it doesn't really come close to what love is supposed to be like.

I guess this year's birthday wasn't much better except that less than a week ago I kissed Sarah for the first time, making it only a twelve year wait. Since being with Sarah, I haven't been able to keep the thought of kissing her off my mind.

Before that, I really couldn't stop thinking about the time I met her and how I felt an amazing connection. She mentions to me and others the time we met, too. Perhaps there really was a connection there.

I had had two shots of rum before we left for Sarah's friend's party. The three of us walked to the party together and, gloating to Eric, I told him he had to get closer to women so they would love him. He had been complaining that the woman he was in love with didn't talk to him anymore. I didn't say that Sarah and I had kissed but I was clearly much more confident and lost some of the jealousy of him since finally kissing Sarah. I felt like she might get flirty with me and we would kiss again. She looked beautiful and I really wanted it to happen.

I didn't talk to Sarah much at the party. I took a few pictures of Eric and together we stole a few shots of someone's alcohol.

I couldn't remember much after that. I remembered the kitchen counter was full of alcohol shots prepared for everyone and after that I remembered standing in the kitchen when Sarah came and told me she was headed downtown to the bar and I couldn't go. "You're sleeping," she said. If I was sleeping, how did I remember it?

She was being tonight. She took me to one of the couches and told me to sleep there. I pushed her out of the way, upset that she wouldn't let me go, grabbed my bottle of wine and drank it as I walked home. Meanwhile, she and Eric got a ride with everyone to the bars downtown.

This morning Eric showed me some of the pictures he took of me. There was one where I was sleeping on the couch and another where I was clearly acting very animated with two bottles of beer in my hands as Sarah looked at me smiling. I couldn't remember either of these things happening. I didn't go to church today because I was feeling too hung over to go.

It was depressing thinking that Sarah didn't stay with me for my birthday. When I woke up I had a cigarette on the porch and there was a small puddle of vomit there. I walked in and my roommate told me to clean it up. I told her it wasn't mine, that it was from a few weeks ago when one of our other roommates had a party.

She asked me if I remembered last night. She said I was lying down sleeping on the porch when she came home at two in the morning. I told her I didn't remember. So, I didn't even make it to my bed last night.

I cleaned up my puke and hoped that Sarah would reply to my text message. The night that she left and spent an hour in Eric's room, he spoke with me afterwards. He said she didn't say anything about me. "You have to be amazing when you see her," is what he told me. I definitely wasn't amazing last night and I really feel jealous that Eric got to spend my birthday with her instead of me. Although, he did tell me he got lost and separated from them at the bar. He couldn't find Sarah and her friends again after that.

    I wanted to sleep off my hangover but I couldn't fall asleep. I kept remembering that I pushed Sarah, leaving on bad terms but I knew we had to rehearse for our next performance at the college. Knowing this, I waited for her response while listening to the song that was playing when we first kissed. I listened to it over and over for hours today, crying.

# Chapter Three

*Tuesday, October 28, 2014*

Last night Sarah was at my place. There's a really strange gap in my memory. I think what happened was she was in a dream I had after she left. It's strange because the time before seeing her last night, I told her I wanted her to stay the night with me sometime. "I don't know when I'll be able to do that," she replied. "Maybe in the winter," I said. And all of a sudden she is in my dreams and it was as if she did stay with me. The last time I slept beside a woman was when I was with Nina in Montreal, twelve years ago. I didn't ask to sleep with women back then. I just did it and didn't think about it.

Maybe somewhere in the lengthy stretch of time between moving on and meeting Sarah, there was a decision to make lying down to sleep beside a woman more important than I had made it before. At the same time, I want it to be important to Sarah too. Sarah and I didn't talk about it much but it seemed appropriate for me to ask. I guess when I slept beside Nina, it was important even though it was completely unappreciated by both of us on the night it happened, despite being over five-hundred kilometers from Toronto. Nina gave me shelter from the cold Montreal weather, so far away from home, although, Toronto wasn't even my home. I had departed from Toronto. That didn't mean it was my home.

I travelled to Ottawa for the night to see Shawn and went to Montreal the next day. When I got to Montreal, I got lost despite spending at least ten hours back in Toronto studying how to get to Nina's place from the Montreal Greyhound station. I remember finding her dorm and being nervous about showing up at her door.

I finally found Nina's building after getting lost. As I approached her door, Nina's friend and acquaintance of mine from our hometown recognized me on the street outside her place. His presence really took my mind away from where it needed to be. His presence didn't help. "Elliot," he told me "you're in the wrong city." "We'll see about that," I thought. Looking back on it, I was probably a muse for Nina, following her lead in the conversation, looking at the posters she guided me to view and holding her guitar that she took out of the closet for me to examine.

I had dreamt the whole way there on the greyhound bus that I would tell her that I loved her when she asked what I was doing there. She did ask me that too, but I didn't say it at the door because I was nervous and then I resolved to tell her when I got to her room. I couldn't do it there either and I didn't all night, not even after she led me back to the bus station the following afternoon and we said goodbye.

I've only seen Sarah's room once. I've stood at her front door longer than I've spent in her room. Her room had so much charm that I wanted to stay there. We were grabbing some beer before we left and got drunk in the park, like we usually did in the summer. I know I hate things that get placed in my room that never get looked at but, since then, I've wanted to buy her something for her room that suits what she already has adorned it with. She'll probably move on from that room and have no desire to keep anything I give her, wherever she goes.

She's been to my place a lot. She was here last night. I played her a song I wrote for her four months ago. I missed her greatly when I wrote it and I was trying to express that being with her had been the most beautiful time for me. We had spent every day together for two weeks except for two days. During the two days we were apart, I wrote that song about what I really felt.

We took a break from rehearsing last night and I let her read the lyrics of the song. She asked me to play it, so I did, and then she asked me to kiss her. After a few minutes into kissing her she stopped and left while telling me the sweetest things I ever heard anyone say.

We were in the middle of kissing in this chair. "Do you know," I asked her, "where I got this chair?" She didn't. "It was given to me by an old guy in my parents' building," I said. "His wife died and he was moving out and he gave it to me. I wonder if they ever did anything in this chair." And we went on kissing.

That man seemed very depressed that his wife had died. We rode down the elevator together, in my parents' building, a couple days after he gave me the chair. He told me he and his wife had seen me play in a big band at the legion. I asked him if they danced. It was a dance band. He told me I talked to him once at a jazz club with a drummer friend we both knew. It's comfortable chair. It has a history. I'm sure he'd be happy for me that I kissed Sarah in that chair. It's possibly the first time anyone made some time in it since his wife died. It made me proud to touch Sarah that way out of respect for the man that lost his girl.

"Are you obsessed with me," she asked "or just infatuated?" I didn't respond. "I think I'm falling in love with you," she said. "I've never been in love before," I told her as we stood at my front door having a cigarette. Sarah took her bike and went home pretty quick after that. With about five beers in me, I went to sleep.

Before I go to bed, I usually remember my day, the highlights in my own life, instead of watching the sports highlights on TV, like a lot of men do. I fell asleep so fast but I remembered it all when I woke up. I remembered Sarah going into my bathroom. As I leaned in to look at her in the mirror I noticed she was flossing her teeth as if she was getting ready for bed. It was just a dream. I texted Sarah in the morning and asked her if she flossed while she was at my place. She didn't. It was just a dream. She wasn't getting ready for bed. She didn't sleep next to me.

When I slept beside Nina that night in Montreal, twelve years ago, I told her I had to put on music to fall asleep. We put on the Leonard Cohen compilation album I brought with me. I fell asleep easily because I was drunk. I'd been drinking Portuguese wine from a little convenience store down the street from her building. I was used to buying any kind of liquor at a government liquor store in Ontario.

I went to the convenience store tonight to buy a pack of cigarettes and the man in front of me was buying a corkscrew. It reminded me of Nina and her dorm. She didn't have a corkscrew, so she asked people in her dorm for one to open my Portuguese wine. I was worried all of her roommates would come join us if they knew we were drinking, but they let us be alone.

I'm still wearing my jacket from when I went to the convenience store tonight. It's so cold now. I don't get to drink with Sarah in the park anymore because of the weather. We drank beer at the playground at the beginning of October, just after we kissed for the first time, just after my birthday. The temperature has been dropping off since the beginning of the fall and so have our outdoor visits. "This is just like the good old days, five months ago," I said to her and she laughed. "Happy five months," she responded. It is tough going to sleep when I'm shivering and the weather is keeping me from doing exciting things every day. I like hockey, maybe I'll watch the highlights tonight.

# Chapter Four

*Friday, November 21, 2014*

Sarah brought us wine and supper. The Thai food had been in her fridge for a couple of days. It was cold when we ate it. I had saved the five beers Sarah left in my room since I saw her a week ago. I'm feeling unable to do the things I want with Sarah. I can't afford to treat her the way I want to since I have no job and only rely on a small disability pension that comes to me once a month. I've heard my dad say it a million times: nothing in this world is free. It's a really ironic statement when the only thing in the world you want is free.

I feel like my heart is collapsible now. It's like one of those cups that you get in a first aid kit that collapses and expands to take pills. Sarah brought the bottle of wine. Sarah brings a cup with her when we drink wine.

When I was a small child and got my first allowance, I was given two quarters from my mother. I needed to spend it immediately. My mother and I took a walk down to the little plaza at the end of the road. As a child who had never been to school yet and only knew the kids that lived on the same block, the plaza seemed like light years away. I couldn't hold on to the quarters long enough to make it to the plaza. I saw a wine glass at a yard sale that struck my fancy. The first thing I ever bought was a wine glass. I had a quarter to spare. To me, it was the Holy Grail I had already known about.

When Sarah left, I gave her a letter to take home with her. When she left, I asked her if I could walk her home and she told me she didn't want me to. I looked at her disappointedly and she looked at me, disappointed that I wouldn't let her be free. She had a bad knee that night and she was wearing a knee brace over her black leggings. Later on in the week I was walking to the plaza at the end of my street and I noticed a knee brace under a bush on the corner. I texted her asking how her knee felt. She said it was feeling better. Then I told her I noticed a knee brace near my house and I asked her if it was hers. She laughed boisterously, in text, and told me she didn't feel like carrying it home when she left, so she threw it away.

Sarah has a job and she can afford knee braces and wine and Thai food. The last time I had a job was four years ago and I hadn't yet met Sarah and I felt a lot more alone than I do now. I went home from the bar with a girl when I still had that job. The bar had closed and a group of us were hanging around outside deciding how to get home.

Many of the straggling few dissipated and my cab had arrived. One of the cute girls waiting there asked me if it was my cab. I told her it was and she asked me to kiss her. She gave me a quick peck on the lips while the cab driver waited for me. She asked me if I could take her home so she came with me. She was a young brown-skinned girl. Arriving at her driveway, I asked her if I should come with her and she said no. The driver stopped.

"Can you pay for it?" she asked, "I have no money." She left and I never saw her again. The cab driver then brought me home with a lecture about women who use men.

I lost my job because I wanted to have a cigarette. I couldn't wait until my break and my manager fired me after I did this a few times, after I was warned. My Zippo lighter is really the only remnant I have of that time in my life when I had something that could be used. I bought that Zippo lighter when I had that job. Now, because I have no money I can't be used but it doesn't matter now because the only thing I want is free.

I was expecting Sarah to come over on Monday this week. When she left last Tuesday she said she would come on Monday. On Sunday, it had been very stressful because I was having trouble memorizing a speech that I had to deliver on Monday afternoon in one of my classes. Sarah had also become slightly unreachable on the weekend and I was wondering if she had lost interest with me. We didn't part on good terms before she left and threw her knee brace away. I remembered ominously the look on the both of our faces as we parted.

I thought I would feel better after my rehearsal but the lack of response to the messages I had sent to Sarah all weekend was making me ache like a junkie without his fix. I couldn't concentrate to study and most of all I wished I could speak to her, or as a consolation, to anyone else. So I called my father.

My father is seventy years old and has had trouble hearing since the tire on his bicycle popped as he was changing it this past summer. He told me to speak up several times as we were on the phone. "I'm sorry," he finally said, "I can't hear you." I became angry with him after that. "Fine," I shouted, "I'll just hang up then!" I hung up the phone. I was so upset I walked over to my parents' apartment.

I brought over my speech and he helped me learn it until after midnight. I needed to be with someone that could help me take my mind away from where it was naturally inclined, or declined, to go. When I got there he gave me some wonderful homemade pizza and carbonated water. It was a luxurious meal that I wasn't used to on my own. He told me I should just stay there for the night. I stayed there that night.

The last time I had slept there for the night was a year ago. I had been in a cold war with Amy, one of the female roommates I live with. I brought her to my room a couple times and the last time she was in my room, I began touching her breasts and her legs and I took off my shirt. She sat there on the edge of my bed without responding. She was frozen there. I didn't like that she made no effort to join me so I stopped. We stopped talking to each other after that night. When I saw her coming and going, we no longer said hello to one another. It was very uncomfortable to live here during that time. I stayed with my parents for two weeks.

In the morning, I woke up and drank another glass of carbonated water and my dad offered me a coffee and asked me if I wanted something to eat. I had had enough luxury. I took nothing more.

I told my dad I was leaving, and he suggested that I grab my phone before I left. I went to get my phone and there were four messages from Sarah. She said she was sorry she had been unreachable for most of the weekend and that she had just broken up with her boyfriend on Sunday night. I went to school and delivered my speech on Monday. It felt good to fulfill my scholarly duties.

Sarah sent me a message saying she couldn't rehearse with me that night because she was still sad about her break-up. I told her I looked forward to seeing her again. When I saw her last night she described to me how she had spent quite some time thinking about how she was going to break up with her boyfriend. She said he made her upset during the break-up and that she was completely certain she was not making any mistake.

When she left she told me she missed me last week. I had missed her within a few minutes of her leaving, even though she refused to let me walk her home.

If she was a drink she'd be called "tidal wave" and she'd be one part seaweed, four parts beautiful scenery, three parts intoxicant, two parts generic juice and some kind of cute garnish. I just hope when all of her is poured into my heart, I don't collapse on her. I want to support her now that she's free.

I'm so used to being hurt by women that I'm expecting that it has nothing to do with me that she broke up with her boyfriend. I'm expecting that she will fall in love with some other man. She is a tidal wave and she can destroy me and tear me to bits at any time. I'm so accustomed to being broken by women that I'd almost like for it to happen again with Sarah. I honestly don't know what it feels like to be in love.

# Chapter Five

*Monday, December 1, 2014*

    Last February I was in Wal-Mart with my friend Vishal who lived down the street. I met him at the college days after he arrived in Canada from India. His accent was quite thick, but his English had improved in the years we had known each other. He graduated college and moved to British Columbia last May, just after I met Sarah. Before he left, he gave me about four-hundred dollars worth of his clothes that he was unable to take on his flight. Since meeting Sarah, I didn't get to spend much time with him.

    One of the last memorable times we spent together, he was buying groceries and I had nothing to do so I went with him. Months before that, in the fall, just after I moved back from staying with my parents for two weeks, I went grocery shopping with a girl I met in a coffee shop. I went on a few dates with her and then she stopped responding to my messages. She seemed perfect for me because she was only two days younger than me. We left Wal-Mart to shop at the sex shop down the street. She liked the idea of going there when I mentioned they had lava lamps. I think she wanted to go to the sex shop because she wanted to get me horny and leave me frustrated. That's probably how most men have left her. I did nothing awful to her but I guess because I'm a man I deserved it. My lava lamp is off right now.

Before Vishal made his way to the checkout, I spotted some Valentine's Day cards in the discount rack. As he was paying for his groceries, he was flirting with the young cashier. I had five dollars left and I was seriously thinking about buying the Valentines. I asked for a little advice from the pretty, young, blonde cashier. I asked her if she thought it was stupid to buy Valentines and hand them out at the college. She told me she thought it was cute because nobody did that anymore. Perhaps she was just being a good salesperson but I believed her. I bought the cards, thirty-two of them.

On Valentine's Day I handed out about five of them. Most of them had my flirty inscriptions on them along with my name, some with my phone number. At the beginning of my Valentine's Day adventure, I was in the college café when I saw two ladies chatting with each other. I wanted to give one to both of them but I didn't have the guts to do it. I could really only see the face of the brunette. The blonde girl was sitting with her back to me. In my mind, I was going through the dialogue I wanted to spew out in an attempt to send them my Valentine's Day love. I just couldn't do it, and they left.

I eventually left the café and went downstairs for a cigarette. As I was standing there smoking, that same brunette from the café came outside and lit a cigarette just a couple meters from me. I guess because she was alone I had a little more confidence. I gave her one of the cards. She told me she had a four year old daughter so I assumed that she had a boyfriend or she was married. I changed the subject to the blonde friend she was with. I asked her if she would give the card to her friend and I asked her what I wrote on the card. She looked at it and read what I had written on that particular card. "To: Random Hottie," it said. I was kind of embarrassed that I had written that but nonetheless she already had it and the gesture was complete. The other four cards I gave out that day were much easier on the nerves.

At the end of the day, I was at the library computers with Vishal, and Harry. Harry was another student at the college who I met through Vishal. They were making fun of me for my Valentine's Day antics. I was starting to feel like it was a waste of time too but as I was sitting there, I received a random instant message on the social network. It turned out to be the blonde girl who had her back to me in the café. Her friend had passed on the Valentine. The blonde was Valerie. She found me online and decided to contact me. We became friends after that.

Valerie didn't tell me she had a boyfriend though. She waited a couple of weeks to tell me that. I got a little attached to the company the pretty, little twenty year old blonde was giving me. She came over one time and chose my clothes for me before school. She didn't like what I was wearing so she watched me change my clothes in my bedroom. It didn't really bother me that she had a boyfriend. She told me how unhappy she was with him.

We smoked cigarettes in her huge red truck outside the school parking lot. We even went to the sex shop together. She bought some sexy clothes there. She kept telling me that her nickname was Princess and she told me I understood "the princess thing." It was some nasty perception she should have men do everything for her, to win her love, buy her things, and treat her like royalty. Her father had bought her the truck, her father bought her a house, her father paid for all of her food, all of her bills, and she spent money on anything she wanted. I almost didn't buy the Valentines because they were three dollars. I only had five and I like to buy coffee every day.

Still, one Thursday morning I met her at the college and we sat in the hallway talking. In my satchel I had my copy of Jack Kerouac's *The Dharma Bums*. I had decided to wait for a Thursday to read her chapter five. It's a chapter where the lead character, Smith, visits his friends' shack in California to participate in yabyum. Yabyum is described in the chapter as a Buddhist ceremony that is essentially an orgy. In the book, the lead character, Smith is shy to take off his clothes even though the twenty year old blonde named Princess is naked and she is convinced of the sacredness of the yabyum ceremony. By the end of the chapter, Princess and Smith are naked in a tub together discussing their plans to do yabyum every Thursday.

So the following Thursday, Valerie told me her boyfriend was out of town and she invited me over to her house. I went there that night and we sat close together watching TV and movies and looking at her pictures until she told me she was tired and wanted to go to bed. I asked her if she wanted me to go to bed with her but she said no. I went home in a freezing cold February blizzard instead. A few weeks later, around St. Patrick's Day, I kissed her on the cheek before she went into her class. She started to become unresponsive to my phone messages on St. Patrick's Day.

I really had become a little attached to the attention I was getting but I had some suspicion that she and her boyfriend were secretly making fun of me together because she was just using me and pretending like we would have some kind of romance together. As the end of the semester was getting close, I wrote a letter to her and left it on her truck. The next day her boyfriend called me and threatened that he was going to break my face. I told him he should use a knife. I had to cash in my chips and look for something else.

I was feeling a little depressed because I had told a few of my friends and Pastor Derek that I was getting involved with Valerie, and my friends were happy for me. I was kind of embarrassed to see them and have to tell them it came to an end and that I was slightly fearful for my life by the end of it.

Normally, every second Wednesday I would go to bible study with Pastor Derek but after I went separate ways with Valerie, I found it difficult to show my face around him so I skipped the next bible study. I was hanging around the college late in the afternoon instead. I went outside to have a cigarette, and I met a new girl. It had been four days since I talked to Valerie.

I don't know if the new girl was there first or if I was. Regardless, I was smoking a cheap native cigarette and I told her they weren't so good. She offered me one of her cigarettes and I took one. My friend Harry ran into the two of us talking for the first time. As we were talking she told a story and in passing she mentioned her name was Sarah.

"Where did you get that shirt?" I quickly remarked. I was shocked that she was wearing the same shirt Nina wore the last time I saw her because I liked Sarah instantly. "I got it at the thrift store," she replied. The three of us were chain smoking for quite a while there. I had Sarah laughing and slapping her knees at my jokes a couple of times.

It was uncanny the way she looked at me. It was like she was scared but I was going to make her feel safe. I've never seen a look like that before in my life—her eyes pierced me. It was getting late and cold and Sarah decided it was time to go home. Harry and I decided to walk her home. All three of us lived close to campus. As we walked her, I wished Harry hadn't joined us and that I could have walked her home alone so I could ask for her number. She looked scared but she looked back at me again like I was making her feel safe. When we got to her street, I said I was going to go another way to get a coffee and I left the two of them.

In my mind I thought I wouldn't see her again until after the summer and by then she would have forgotten that we even met. I kept walking and then I turned back. I was going to chase after them but I saw Harry had turned back too. I couldn't go after her because I would scare her and she may have been home already. Harry didn't see me watching him, he just walked by and I went to get a coffee.

I saw Harry again on Friday at our friend Rich's house. We talked about meeting Sarah. He got her number and he asked if I wanted it. "Why would you do that?" I asked him. "People have done that for me," he replied. I still couldn't believe he had given me her number.

I waited until the following Friday to send her a message. I didn't want her to be busy with school so I could ask her to come see me that night. I just didn't know if I should or not, but mostly I felt like the way she looked at me and that she was laughing at my jokes and because we walked her home, it was likely that she would see me.

The day I sent her a message, she met me where I left her and Harry the night we first met. We didn't know what we were going to do at first but we eventually went to the college and sat on a picnic table to talk. As we walked to the college she told me she was going to her friend's birthday party. She told me she was twenty years old. I told her I hoped she was older because I was thirty-one. It was strange, but in saying that, she understood immediately that I liked her. We couldn't decide where we were going at first. It was very impromptu.

I told her I was a musician and she told me she was an actress. I told her I played jazz and she told me she did improv sketches. She told me about method acting and as we sat on the picnic table, I noticed she was inching away from me. It was the opposite of the night we met because that first night I had been sitting about a meter and a half away from her but by the time we got up to walk her home, she was only a couple feet away from me. The picnic table was leaning in the direction she was moving. It looked like she was falling. I didn't realize it at the time, but now I'm certain that she had already been drunk that first time we met.

I was expecting her to have to go to the party and I was waiting to find out which way she was going. When she told me where the birthday party was, I realized it was towards my parents' house. I told her I could walk her and that I would visit my parents to watch the hockey game. I asked her if it was okay to walk her to the party and she said yes but she had to go to the washroom first. We went inside the college and she asked me to watch her longboard while she went to the washroom.

As I walked her to her friend's place, she told me about music she liked and we talked about evolution. I told her I thought we evolved from dinosaurs. She knew I was kidding. By this time, it had been about a month since I kissed Valerie on the cheek and I had been hoping to kiss Valerie again soon but I couldn't anymore. When we reached her friend's street, Sarah turned towards me and I knew she was going to give me a hug. I had been thinking that it took me more than a month to kiss Valerie so

I decided that I would kiss Sarah right away instead. After we hugged, as our bodies were pulling away from each other, I held her arms so she would stay still and I kissed Sarah on the cheek.

She looked at me again like she looked at me the first night we met. She looked at me like she was scared but it was okay because it was me. I think she saw that I was scared and she was just looking at me the way I looked at her. I don't know why, but I smiled and laughed all the way to my parents' place after she was gone. We had made plans to sing karaoke together when we were singing The Beatles' *Don't Let Me Down* on the street as I walked her to the party. I felt nothing for Valerie after that night.

I continued to see her at playgrounds where we listened to music, admiring each other and the wonderful spring weather. At first, it surprised me that she always brought beer or wine with her on those first times together. The alcoholism was slightly troublesome but there was a pleasing consistency to the frequency of our meetings. It happened that we regularly met every six days, and I began noticing this pattern. It made me happy that she couldn't go an entire week without asking to see me.

Initially I didn't drink with her, and actually felt bad that all she wanted to do was drink alcohol with me, but I eventually got used to it, joined her, and we made an arrangement to meet at my place to get totally drunk one evening in May.

I had a twenty-sixer of vodka that we mixed with soda and juice. We got to the bottom of the vodka before it was dark. Sarah had about ten dollars and I had about fifteen. We had just enough money to travel to the beer store and get more alcohol. Before the bus came we each had a beer, sitting on a ledge at the side of the road. That moment definitively set the tone of our relationship, and I fell, lovingly, into it.

We finished off those beers at my place, but before the night was over, Sarah was in such high spirits, listening to Mac DeMarco and all kinds of music I had never heard before, that she wanted to dance. "Dance with me," she asked. I felt calm. "I'll join you on a slow one," I replied.

Soon enough, she played a slow one. Slow dances are quite intimate, especially when you're alone in a room together, so I was expecting she may not take me up on my offer. However, I was elated when she said, "Come."

As we were dancing, I lowered my head onto her shoulder and she began sucking on my ear. I took my head away from her shoulder because it bothered me terribly, since she had a boyfriend, that she would do such a thing. It had been such a long time since I kissed a woman, so when she started to feel my chest, it angered me so much that I had the patience to hold back my superfluous desire to kiss her.

After dancing, we sat on my bed listening to more music. "I need something to write on," she said. She grabbed a piece of scrap paper that was on my desk. "No! Use this," I said, and handed her my little blue diary. She wrote something then handed it back to me. "I'll save it for tomorrow," I said.

That's how I met Sarah Benton.

# Chapter Six

*Wednesday, December 24 & Friday, December 26, 2014*

Almost three weeks have passed so quickly. Sarah and I were busy playing music together for a while. By myself, I noticed I buy a lot of coffee. Sometimes I buy two coffees a day. Tim Horton's is just down the street from me, on the corner, but I don't go there much. I go to the little convenience store right next to it. I save about a dollar every time I buy a coffee there instead of Tim Horton's. By the end of the week, if I've bought fourteen coffees, I end up with an extra fourteen dollars in my pocket. Tonight I went there for a coffee and walked around my neighbourhood. I do this every night when I'm alone.

It happens to me frequently when I'm walking at night under all of the streetlights that my shadow is cast on the pavement, sometimes in more than one direction. But occasionally, I'll be walking under the lights and as I transition between the light of one lamp and another, the shadow trailing me seems to creep up quickly behind me, and I think someone is running after me. I look back fearfully and no one's there.

I paid a dollar for the eighty-five cent coffee and I got a nickel in change. I asked the cashier where the extra dime was. As if some kind of magic had taken place, I looked back at the nickel in my hand and there was a dime there too. The cashier winked at me.

I remember sitting in the first home I recall as a child, lying on my father as he sat and watched Wayne Gretzky with the Edmonton Oilers late at night. I usually was put to bed by my mother and I couldn't fall asleep so I'd sneak downstairs and fall asleep on top of my father. One night before I fell asleep, my father showed me a magic trick. A quarter mysteriously disappeared and he made it reappear behind my ear.

One of the most vivid memories I have as a young child with my father was asking him why a quarter was called a quarter. The strange thing is: I seemed to understand him after he explained it. He explained it once and I couldn't concentrate, but he recognized I couldn't understand so he brought me into the bathroom and took an envelope from the hall closet and drew a picture of a dollar bill and four quarters on it. I looked at it and understood in that moment a fourth of any whole is a quarter. In the same way, like a curious child, my father asks me why music notes are named with certain letters. Really, it's a completely arbitrary measure. So are most words. As I walked the streets I put my thoughts together in words, and I realized I'm stuck in my head. We're all stuck in our own heads.

On top of being stuck in my head, whether it's the state of my spirit, or if it's even less meaningful than that, I'm alone, lonely and feel like Sarah is going someplace without me. She went to Toronto last weekend and she's going next weekend too. Christmas is this week and I've been finished my most recent semester of college for a week now. Since the college has closed, Sarah and I haven't been able to perform music at the college bar. We started playing music together there in September.

As time went by, it became kind of a pastime for the two of us, like couples who play bridge, or canasta, or board games, or drink alcohol, take drugs, or go to restaurants. She comes over after discussing on the phone what songs we want to work on, then we work on them for most of the week. Sarah gets excited to play them with me. I don't quite understand how she could be so excited to play music all the time. I've been performing music in restaurants, bars, coffee shops and parties for almost fifteen years and have had almost no success with it. To me, going to perform songs at the college twice every month is a complete waste of time. Nowadays, the performance aspect of music heightens my anxiety.

I just play guitar and Sarah is a beautiful woman with a fantastic singing voice so when we go up there and perform, usually a guy will try to get her number and tell her she's a great singer. Meanwhile, the guitar shackles both my hands together on the nights I'm performing with Sarah. Two weeks before she broke up with her boyfriend, she met one of the performers as we were leaving. His name is Blake and he took her number right in front of me just before we left. We left and I told her I wanted to smash my guitar over his head.

She told me he had been inviting her out to go for drinks so the next time we performed she got a ride home with him and I left without her. He performed an original song that revolved around the idea of two men sleeping with the same woman. I came home and smoked pot with the guy that lives in the basement and drank a beer with Eric, my neighbour.

The next weekend, she came over and I kissed her. "You're so sexy," I said, "I feel like I can't touch you." She didn't kiss me back. She looked at me like she wanted to touch, and a few minutes later she asked me if she could stay over. We went to the corner for a slice of pizza and she told me then that I could touch her. We came home and we fell asleep in our undergarments.

I woke up in the morning before her, sat in my chair beside the bed where she lay, and I listened to a song that had a title that described Sarah and I cried. I hadn't heard it in a long time and the lyrics set off my emotions. I don't know if it was the lyrics or if I was happy or sad. "The most beautiful woman in the world is asleep in my bed right now," I thought.

The next time we performed I told her I didn't want to go. I didn't want to see that guy she'd been talking to. I didn't say that, but regardless, she called me an ass and I told her I wasn't so she retorted by calling me selfish and told me she always has to put up with me and I always flake out on her. I didn't want to be selfish so I went. Blake was performing as we walked near the bar. We could hear him singing and playing guitar as we walked through the halls of the college towards the stage. Sarah got very excited that he was playing.

By the time we reached the bar, I told her I didn't want to perform anymore. We didn't talk for a few minutes. Then she tried to convince me to play. When she told me she loved me, it sounded like she was saying I hate you. She wasn't saying what she really felt and neither was I. Before she went outside to have a cigarette, I told her I would play and she said she didn't want to if I didn't want to. She came back in from having a cigarette and immediately asked me what songs we were going to play. Blake had already left.

We performed our songs. It was our worst performance since we started in September. Sarah was intoxicated beyond relief and both of us were upset with each other and we both wanted to go home. I was so upset with her. She apologized to me before we left and in the morning I sent her a message saying I loved her.

I really hated her. Now I'm stuck in my head, and my apprehension for doing what makes Sarah happy is causing her to go somewhere without me. I hate what makes her happy. How could she love me now?

~ ~ ~

In another way, I feel like it's laziness to refuse to play music with her. I feel like sometimes I'm a little stuck sitting under a tree thinking I'm the Buddha. Just now a friend on the social network shared a quote from the Buddha. "We are shaped by our thoughts. We become what we think. When the mind is pure, joy follows like a shadow that never leaves," it says.

I found a new spot while walking, where a path leads into a park that is completely closed-in by houses and the fences at the ends of peoples' backyards. I walked by it the other day when I saw my shadow. It felt like those childish moments when you're upset and in a tantrum so someone makes a joke to cheer you up and it's funny but you just don't budge from being upset.

In a warmer mood, I walked into that park today and sat there and thought I'd like to take Sarah there, maybe a month after the groundhog sees *his* shadow. Right now, we can't because a large amount of snowfall is impending.

I need to do what's right and make Sarah happy. She's finished her work term from her college job placement. In a few months her savings will be slightly depleted and her lifestyle will change. Who knows? Maybe she will find a new job but she won't be working five days a week anymore because she starts college classes again in the next semester.

I need to play music with her. I don't want to sit under a tree, alone thinking about what could be. Sitting in that new spot, my new favourite spot, I thought of the time she was playing a song loudly on her phone, walking to the plaza and when we got to the plaza another girl saw her dancing to it and joined. The two of them danced together in the plaza parking lot while another girl videotaped them. I thought I'd tell our children that story.

The thought that I've slept beside her has made me just as happy. In the middle of the night I woke up and she was beside me lying on her side. I stroked my hand lightly across her body from her shoulder to her hip. I had so much desire for her at that very moment, in her peaceful state. When I went back to sleep, I dreamt that I was drifting in the sky with a beautiful woman. I couldn't tell who she was. We were both naked and I was getting closer to her as we both floated there in the atmosphere. I realized it was Sarah, although it didn't look like Sarah. The closer I got, as if I was trying to penetrate her with my erection, the farther she floated away. It was a strange tease for me.

I spent the entire morning with Sarah. She woke up around ten-thirty after I had listened to some music, showered, and cried a bit. We went for breakfast and then we got a coffee. She told me that she had a dream that I was touching her and getting sexual with her. "Did you?" she asked. "No," I lied. "Elliot Stephenson," she said, "sleeps with women, but doesn't fuck them." Then she told me about her other dreams but that's the one I remember her telling me about.

I feel so happy most days. I'll be staring into space, without a thought in my head, then all of a sudden I remember something like that time she danced with the girl at the plaza and I will start to laugh out loud. But, I think that because I'm so happy, the easiest, most minute bit of sadness will strike me like it is the hardest blow anyone has ever endured.

In a few moments I will walk out my door, I will turn left around the bend, continue down Newton Street, past the streetlights, past another set of streetlights, and continue down our street to her house. I will have my acoustic guitar with me and I will get to her door and she will be there to sing with me. We will practice, and who knows what else? Her parents have left for winter vacation. They went to Texas. I have missed Sarah since the second after she closed her door when I left her place the last time.

# Chapter Seven

*Saturday, December 27, 2014*

I didn't knock on Sarah's door when I got there. I felt like I was intruding. I felt like she wouldn't really want to see me anyway. I got to her door, I didn't knock, then I walked down the street back home. It reminded me of something that happened eleven or twelve years ago. The only difference was, I had no anxiety in the beginning and I was in love with Nina. Victoria was one of Nina's best friends and she lived in Toronto when I was also living there.

Victoria, I thought, was with me in my love for music that reeked of obsolescence. "How are you doing in your retirement?" she asked me one time at her dorm when I was twenty years old. Victoria picked up right where I left off with Alaina. Alaina had given me the Leonard Cohen novel, *The Favourite Game*, two years before, and the morning after I slept beside Victoria she told me her favourite Leonard Cohen song was *Famous Blue Raincoat*. Nobody had a favourite Leonard Cohen song and nobody liked Oscar Peterson for that matter either. It's asking for an early retirement to play music like that these days.

We listened to it in her dorm the next year, all year. I didn't love her. She was insecure and she insulted me because she thought that I would never love her. She would never discuss her favourite things, only what she didn't like. We never knew where to go. Finding dinner on dates was always an exercise in excessive peregrination. Yonge Street in Toronto is a long street when you don't know where you're going. We always resolved to hit up the jazz club near Osgoode Station. By the third time this happened that year, I refused to go there because it was turning into a cliché so we just turned around and ate at some dive near Ryerson University instead.

It was a bit of a chore to go visit Victoria at her dorm. It took me forty-five minutes by bus and subway. I repeatedly saw the same young woman sitting across from me on subway trips. I found out later her name was Christine. I didn't talk to her for the first few of the many times I saw her and noticed she was becoming a fixture of my subway rides but we looked at each other.

In the last of my days living in Toronto, I was going to the southeast part of the city to go see some jazz music. I was meeting a few of my old friends down there. I was riding the subway and it stopped, a voice came over the speaker instructing the passengers there was a problem with the train and we'd have to get off and wait for the next one. When the next one came, on it were my friends I was headed to meet.

I often took the streetcar down to the jazz club too. It was one ride. I didn't have to transfer. One summer, I was headed down to the club and I spotted a girl from my hometown walking down the street. It was the last woman I kissed before Sarah. I quickly got off the streetcar, crossed the street and caught up to her and her two friends that I had never met before.

I met Lella that day. Soon after I left Toronto, Lella came and talked to me at my old hangout in my hometown and we ended up talking all night. We ended up taking a university class together a couple years later in my hometown. I caught her again, in happenstance, at a subway entrance in Toronto just a few years ago. She told me she was getting married.

Every Friday I'd go see the jazz singer, Melissa Santos, sing at the jazz club. I originally went because it was listed on the music schedule that she had a guitarist in the band. I never once saw that guitar player play with her. I tried to see that guitar player several more times and never once was he there. Melissa was also a waitress at the bar. Not only did I like her singing but I found her extremely attractive, even though I was twenty and she was probably fifteen or twenty years older than me. She hadn't talked to me and I hadn't tried to talk to her.

One Friday night in December, I saw Melissa coming near the bar where I was sitting. I guess I was looking at her so she said hi to me. "Hi," I said, "I like your singing, would you go for coffee and pie with me?" "I don't do that," she replied. I was so proud of myself for asking her to go out with me and even though in any other circumstance, her decline would have been a broadsword to the flesh, she hadn't upset me in the slightest. I finished my four pints of Amsterdam Blonde, as per usual, and left the bar just before ten o'clock.

I was elated by asking Melissa on a date so I decided I'd take a drunken ice skate at city hall. After that, I went back to see Victoria at Annesly Hall which was her dorm at the university.

We went out to the little bar just around the corner. I was in a good mood all night.

I caught the subway back home from St. George Station and I saw the drummer from my band. We didn't talk much, it was kind of just a gig for both of us, but he gave me a surreptitious nose tap as he glanced and nodded my way. Soon after, my 'Miss Coincidence' walked through the subway door right in front of me. She looked at me and looked to sit across from me but instead she sat right beside me, leaving a seat between us. I looked at her and didn't say anything and she looked at me too. Her face was blank and emotionless. After a couple of stops went by, I smiled, shook my head a little and I greeted her.

We introduced ourselves, and we admitted it was odd for both of us to see each other so consistently on the subway. She was going to High Park Station and she was also a student and her name was Christine. I couldn't really concentrate too much on anything because I was far beyond my normal alcohol intake level after having a few more pints with Victoria. I must have seemed crazy to Christine.

As we heard the announcement for the next stop I puked right in the middle of the subway floor. She asked me if I was okay and I don't remember much of what Christine did after that. She got off the subway and luckily enough it wasn't the last time I saw her. On the other hand, I did fall asleep, missed my stop at Royal York Station missing the last southbound bus. Instead I went to Islington Station, caught the all-night bus southbound and had to walk about thirty minutes home.

I went to my hometown for the Christmas break soon after. When I got back to Toronto in January, I went to visit Nina in Montreal. I spent all the money I had for the month by going to visit Nina in Montreal that January. I borrowed Victoria's portable CD player for the Greyhound ride.

In the summer after that, before I left Toronto, I was asked by Victoria to take care of her mother's garden for the weekend while she and her family went away. I watered the flowers on the first day. It was very hot and sunny both days I was there. On the second day, I walked in the house and went out back to the garden where I noticed the roses had burned. In that moment I became very sick and had trouble thinking clearly and decided I should go to the hospital. Before I left, I wrote a letter to apologize for the roses and explained that I had to go to the hospital. I didn't know what was wrong with me.

They kept me in the hospital for the rest of the day. Waiting for the doctor, I noticed a clear plastic basket that was being ignored by the doctors and nurses and patients. One of the nurses instructed me to wait for the doctor in one of the rooms. "Wait in here," she instructed, "the doctor will be with you shortly." I stood there in awe, looking at what was in the basket. It was a breathing, bony hump of flesh that looked like a two foot by two foot fried chicken thigh with short, fine brown hair growing all over its skin. I thought it was God. I was scared, and confused. The basket had tubes attached to it, connected to a large machine, both behind the nurse standing in front of me. I stared at it, confused, thinking God must have been in critical care.

"Oh, you're wondering about that? Don't worry about that, that's Eddie," she said, "the doctor will be with you momentarily." I waited in the room, and the doctor came. He asked me if I was on any medications. I wasn't. I began seeing his credentials and his name hovering in front of his face as if I was watching him on a television screen. I was very confused. He was right in front of me, I was seeing him on TV and I had just seen God.

They let me out of the hospital at dusk. I took the bus back into Toronto to catch the bus home. I walked past Christine without noticing her. I sat down on the bus and I realized that she was there as I looked at her through the window. I don't know if she noticed me, but I never saw her again and I don't even remember what she looks like now.

Victoria told me she fucked her ex-boyfriend just a few hours before my twenty-second birthday party and we stayed friends until I moved back to my hometown the next spring. I don't remember anything about the last time I saw her. I didn't know it was going to be the last time. I just remember showing up at her door one day after work and nobody answered. I could hear her talking to her roommate and the television in the background. I gave up I guess. There wasn't much thought behind it. I haven't seen her big blue eyes since. For some reason I was reminded of all this. Now I don't remember why.

My thoughts were not normal for about four years after. When I moved back to my hometown, after two years of living in Toronto, I kept thinking I was living across from a Petro-Canada station in Edmonton and could smell gasoline all the time, even though the nearest gas station was an Esso station several blocks away and I was most certainly living in Northern Ontario. It was a permanent conundrum in my mind until I started to write. As I continued to write, my mind became clearer. I started writing almost ten years ago, a year after I moved home from Toronto and since then, I haven't stopped.

# Chapter Eight

*Monday, February 2, 2015*

The winter is not good for me. I find my hands get cold, and the agility of my fingers is compromised by the weather. In the fall, a year ago, at the cusp of winter my anxiety was rising. I became very depressed. I hadn't been intimate with a woman in seven years and I was packing up my spirit to hibernate after Amy, my roommate, decided she wasn't going to participate when I tried becoming romantic with her. Last year, same as this year, I was also getting ready to move my spirit into my room, so it didn't freeze. It's a cold, cold world out there even when it's just ten degrees below zero.

It was the end of November, just over a year ago. I couldn't sleep at night. I began crying every day. I called up Pastor Derek and told him how much I missed Alaina and Nina. He didn't understand. Those two women were part of my life ten to twelve years ago. He's only been in my life for the past four years. The next night I called my sister a couple of hours past midnight, and there was no answer. My sister wasn't talking to me much. She never does unless I initiate a conversation with her. My anxiety kept me up through the wee small hours of the morning. My anxiety coaxed me to walk to her door at the crack of dawn.

I sat on the bench on her porch talking to myself. Soon enough, I saw my sister and her husband dressing their daughter for school. I guess they heard me talking to myself and her husband came outside. He asked me if I was high a couple of times. I hadn't drunk alcohol since the beginning of September, or likewise taken any pot. Actually, because my nearest friend was Pastor Derek, I had only drunk alcohol one time in the two years prior. I hadn't taken any drugs in even longer. I wasn't intoxicated, yet I wasn't making any sense. My sister came outside and asked me if I was hungry. I was hungry, in more ways than one. She gave me two pieces of toast and an apple. She called my father and my sister's husband took me and my father to see my doctor.

When we got there, my doctor told my father I had to be restrained and I needed to go to the hospital. My father agreed and I tried to leave but my father wouldn't let me so I ended up in the psycho ward at a hospital just north of Toronto. I refused to let them give me a needle to take my blood for almost an hour. I'm afraid of needles. Soon after, I gave in and gave my blood. They found me a room with a bed and I met some of the other young, crazy people the hospital had to offer at the time. I didn't get restrained.

I met Jonathan that night. He told me that we should be roommates. He was terrifically funny, like someone from a movie or a late night talk show. He told me about the illegal drugs he had taken in the past. He told me he does stand-up comedy. In the morning I met Laurel. She had blonde hair and blue eyes, was very cute and subtle and had an Englishman husband who visited at nights. I spent every morning there talking to her.

When I was there, I was on drugs day and night. I don't know what they were giving me but I slept every night by eleven and woke up before seven to meet with Laurel.

Soon after, I met Rebecca. She was tall and skinny with brown hair and tanned skin. She looked like a model, was very fun and seemed quite happy but showed some undertones of a lasting depression. In any event, the group of us and some others made the best of our time in that hospital. It was like a movie, set in a psych ward of a hospital. None of us were crazy. There was nothing wrong with any of us. We were all just broken a little on the inside, somehow.

A couple days later, I borrowed some hand lotion from Laurel. A little later, as she walked by I held out my finger with a dab of it. She took it off my finger and went into her room. I couldn't stop laughing, thinking how funny that was, like we were characters from *1984* and hand lotion had been banned.

The food there was nice. I didn't smoke one cigarette for the week I was there. One morning, someone brought donuts from the outside and I appreciated it. More than anything, things like that are special when your freedom is compromised and you appreciate the special parts of life more. It's really disgusting how much we take for granted when we have everything you could ask for, and more.

We did yoga classes some afternoons, we put puzzles together with a group that came in and one day they brought in some video games and nobody showed up to play except for Rebecca and me. I told Rebecca I didn't care about winning. We had a good time even though neither of us played video games in our real lives. For the most part, I wanted to go home but for whatever reason there was a bond that occurred between a few of us in that hospital, that week that we were together.

The day before Rebecca left, I was talking to Laurel in the seats where we talked every morning, and I got up to get my things to have a shower. On the way to my room I ran into Rebecca. We talked for a couple of seconds, I don't remember what she said but then she opened the opening in the front of her hospital pants and showed me her vagina. "Could you imagine that?" she said. I quickly responded, "Yeah, I can imagine that." Before she left, I wrote down my e-mail address and gave it to her. I haven't talked to her since.

I talked to Jonathan about getting a car and visiting him. He lived near the hospital. I couldn't afford a car, had no job, and could barely make ends meet with my disability check. There were some local magazines with ads for cars placed in the hospital by people who lived around that part of Southern Ontario. I also spent time looking at apartments in the area. I wanted to be closer to these new friends I made.

Before I left that hospital, I asked Jonathan and Laurel to contact me. I had removed myself from the social network for four months so they weren't able keep in contact with me that way but I gave them my e-mail address and they gave me theirs. I was being sent to the psych unit at the hospital where I live so my parents could visit me easier. Finally, I was released on a stretcher into the back of an ambulance that took me to the hospital near my house. I didn't even get to have a cigarette.

The food was worse in the new hospital and there were a lot of older people. When I got there I masturbated for the first time in a week. When I first arrived, I was placed in an observation room that looked right out into the nurses station and I was turned on by the exhibitionism of masturbating in a room visible to them.

After a couple days, I met a girl named Catherine who had just arrived. We spent the mornings together there. I was having trouble sleeping again when I got there and I was craving a cigarette quite a bit. They let me outside once while I was there but I had no cigarettes so going outside seemed to be a waste of time.

Eventually, I got to talking to Catherine one night alone in the cafeteria. "Come closer," she said as she was talking to me. So I moved my face closer to hers. "A little closer," she said. Then I moved closer so my lips were only an inch or two from hers. It would have been so nice. I couldn't do it. I have no confidence, I think I am ugly and women don't like me. I moved back away. "That's what I thought," she said in her charming English accent.

My parents visited every night, bringing me the best food I'd had in weeks—chicken wraps, burritos, trail mix, cola, cookies, muffins. It was amazing to have them nearby. While I was there, I started using the social network again. There was a computer with internet that patients had to share. After about two weeks there, they were ready to release me. Because I hadn't spent all of my money at the beginning of December, it was the first time I actually made ends meet. I had about eighty dollars left and I had just got my check for January.

The first thing I did when I was free again was buy some clothes. I bought a hoody sweater and a pair of red pants. I didn't wear the pants until the spring, after I met Sarah. Eventually, last fall, those pants were my lucky pants. Four out of the five times that I was with her romantically I was wearing those red pants. I knew they were special the day I bought them.

So as December was coming to an end last year, I became friends with Laurel and Jonathan on the social network. The two of them were still in hospitals for a little while longer than me. After I met Valerie on Valentine's Day last year, I talked to Laurel quite a bit. Because of the incidents with Catherine and Rebecca, I think I got a little more confidence and thought maybe women might actually like me more than I assumed. It was the closest I had been to kissing a woman in eleven years. I regretted not having the courage in the hospital and I needed another chance soon.

I really like that when you're in your thirties, you get to know some married people. Married people are in lasting relationships, and aren't worried about losing their partners. I tend to prefer talking to married people about relationships more than anyone else. And least of all do I like talking to my male friends about relationships. They just go behind your back. Shawn is married, so is Pastor Derek, and so is Laurel. I hadn't talked to Laurel in a year but about two months ago I talked to her about Sarah. She invited me to come see her in Richmond Hill. I never did but it created a simple twist of fate as Bob Dylan put it.

I was supposed to go to church on Sunday but I had made plans to go to Richmond Hill to see Laurel. On Sunday, I sent Laurel a message asking if we were still going to meet but she said she was busy building a yoga studio with her husband. Her husband now invites me to come see both of them. He says he wants me to play guitar for them. I had already told Pastor Derek I had other plans and couldn't come to church so he didn't pick me up. At the end of December, the weather wasn't quite as bad as it is now and I was occasionally still going for walks. That Sunday it was only ten degrees below zero which was notably warmer than it had been so I went for a walk. I think I may have walked past Sarah's house that afternoon but I can't remember completely. Church usually ends around five-thirty in the afternoon and I get back by six o'clock.

As I was arriving home from my walk around four o'clock, I noticed Amy and her sister, Anna, standing at the front door having cigarettes. Amy and I hadn't talked much since the incident when I felt her up. I met her and her sister in June when Amy and I were looking to rent the rooms of our house almost two years ago.

As I walked up to the door, that Sunday afternoon, Anna, my roommate's sister asked me to give her a hug. She hugged me a little longer than I was accustomed to a hug's duration being. She then talked to me for a couple minutes while my roommate went back inside. That's when Anna asked me to pick her up. So I grabbed her and she jumped on me, wrapping her legs around my waist. Her face was close to mine and we kissed there on the steps. I looked around to see if Eric saw us. He didn't see us kissing. We began kissing deeply for a while longer. She told me she liked me since we first met and I told her I liked her then, too. My roommate came back outside as the two of us were making out on the step and I stopped. "I can't do this," I said and went back inside.

I hadn't had a shower in two days. Sometimes when I don't see Sarah for a while, I don't take good care of myself. It was the Christmas break from school so I didn't really have anything else going on other than seeing Sarah occasionally. I sat in my room very pleased but kind of anxious because I really wished I had just kissed Sarah again. I thought that I wouldn't have kissed Anna if I went to church that day. I would have missed her if I came home at six o'clock. I started thinking of how nice it would have been if I had let it progress naturally instead of stopping it.

Somebody knocked on my door a few minutes later, though. I think it was Anna but I don't know for sure because I didn't answer the door. After the person left, I sat in Tim Horton's for a few hours. I wanted very badly to run into the arms of Sarah. We weren't like that and I couldn't just go knocking on her door whenever I felt like it, even though her parents were away in Texas. I sat in Tim Horton's messaging my sister on my phone about what happened. I felt good though, better than I had been. Still, I am sorry. Anything ever written needs a disclaimer.

I was alone on New Year's Eve. Anna was at the house with her sister drinking and having fun. We didn't talk though. School started soon after and I saw Sarah at the college the first Friday she was back. It was odd but it was good. I began seeing her with a lot of her college friends and I was too shy to talk to her in such large groups. I think sometimes she doesn't really want me around but when I'm feeling right, something tells me it isn't a correct assessment to think that.

I became very poor in the early weeks of January. I had spent all my money and I was relying on my parents to give me some money until my first work check came in. I started work on the eleventh of January and my parents had given me eighty dollars in case I needed to take cab rides to work. I had almost run through all of that money after my first week of work so I decided I would take some empty beer and liquor bottles back for refunds. I gathered all of the empty bottles and placed them by the door and went out for a cigarette. Anna was outside on the step having a cigarette. I told her there was a mess inside because the entrance was full of empty bottles I was taking back. She went inside.

I finished my cigarette and when I came back inside Anna had come back upstairs to ask me if I would buy her some beer when I went brought back the empty bottles. She handed me twenty dollars and she told me what she wanted me to buy for her. I was making some food while waiting for the next bus. After I ate, I got ready and carried all of the clunking empty bottles in a backpack and a bag in each hand. They didn't have what Anna asked for but I got her something else instead.

My parents live close to the beer store so I went over to see them while I waited for the bus home. I had been gone for about an hour and a half before arriving home. Anna was expecting me so she waited for me at the door. I gave her the beers and she told me I could keep the four dollars change. I went back to my room. A few minutes later I went back out for a cigarette and as I was going outside, Anna was there again. She told me her sister had fallen asleep and she wanted me to keep her company in my room. I agreed and we both went out for a cigarette first.

She explained to me that she didn't want to make noise while her sister was sleeping. None of this seemed out of the ordinary. We began talking about the time we kissed almost a month earlier and we both reaffirmed that we felt a connection the first time we met, the time Amy and I were looking to rent the place. "I'm going to rape you," Anna said to me quite bluntly as we stayed out there for a second cigarette. I thought about it but I didn't think for very long. "Yeah, we can do that," I replied.

We came inside, and began kissing on my bed. It felt strange not knowing her very well. She told me I had small kisses. Sarah has small lips; I was used to her little mouth. Anna told me I would love her until it drove me crazy. She went to the bathroom, and then she came back and I went to the bathroom and

I brushed my teeth. I liked looking at her topless body when I came back. We kissed again and she told me she liked my minty breath. She began to take off her pants and I quickly took off mine along with her and then April looked in December, the month following Monday.

I enjoyed the feeling of the sex with her but I couldn't remember her name. I almost called her Sarah a few times. The moments after the sex with her, holding her naked body, feeling without inhibition, satisfied and calm for a seemingly endless amount of time were the best parts. I wanted her to leave when she began telling me about a guy that she was still in love with. She missed him. I suppose that would have hurt my feelings if I didn't feel the same way about Sarah.

I woke up beside Anna the next day and had to make her leave because I had a class at noon. She left, I went to class and then I came home and washed my bed sheets. When I went down to the laundry room to put my sheets in the dryer, Anna was in the laundry room with another guy. Her sister told me I shouldn't go in there because Anna was. I could hear the sounds of her love making coming from inside. I went back upstairs and brought my sheets back later.

That night, I went to see Sarah for the first time in about two weeks. I didn't tell her what had happened. We danced with her friend to Cyndi Lauper and they drank wine. I had one drink and we played some of our old repertoire. After a few hours, Sarah and her friend were pretty drunk and tired so I decided I would leave. Sarah walked me out. "Sorry," she said just before I put on my shoes to leave. "Why?" I asked. She didn't say why but I put on my shoes, we said goodbye, and I walked home.

The following Sunday, I went to church for the first time in a long time. Once a month, the church has its service at a coffee shop downtown. Instead of a normal service, they have kind of a little open mic with musicians, and sometimes poetry, mixed in with a little bit of preaching. One guy who I had met before got up to play a song. I listened to the lyrics and liked the beginning of his song. As it turns out it was the Bob Dylan song *A Simple Twist of Fate*. In that very moment it was quite fitting for me. To remember being with Anna, I bought with my first pay check a turntable and a vinyl record that had that song on it. I kind of liked the twist of fate.

# Chapter Nine

*Sunday, February, 15, 2015*

Yesterday was Valentine's Day. I was alone. About a week ago, I had planned to go to see some bands downtown. On the thirteenth, Sarah decided she was going to go to the show too. I've been feeling weird seeing her at the college lately. Since I've known her, she had been working at a job placement for college and I never actually saw her at school. Now, every time I see her she's with a bunch of people from her classes and I feel too insecure to go and say hi. I felt like that last night. If she was going to be at the show, I'd probably feel too awkward to talk to her, so I didn't go.

I ended up talking to my sister on the phone. My sister fell asleep talking to me. She was very tired from putting her daughter to bed. I was right in the middle of telling her about how great the summer was with Sarah and how it has changed and now I never see her. I thought of the first time I ever slept beside a woman. Stephanie said the sweetest things any girl has ever said to me until I met Sarah. That night I slept beside Stephanie,

I kept talking in a dulcet voice, in hopes that I would lull her to sleep. I told her if I asked her a question that she was not to respond to me, that she was to just listen and that way she would fall asleep. Still, she answered every question I asked her. I don't remember falling asleep but we did, together.

That was the last time I slept beside Stephanie. I've always felt that sleeping with someone is the most pleasurable thing you can share together. It's the most comfortable thing I can think of doing, it's the most natural thing you do that has some kind of beauty to it. For someone to just want to be near you and not need to laugh, or try, or have an orgasm, and just need comfort, it's one of the greatest gestures you can send someone's way. Maybe sometimes it means nothing, although I always sleep better next to someone.

When I was a teenager, my friends would come over and I would fall asleep while they watched television. I was watching the St. Louis Cardinals game one time with my old buddy, Brady, and I went to sleep. I woke up with Brady jumping on top of me when Mark McGwire hit his sixty-second home run that season. I feel very lonely when I sleep alone. Most nights, what I desire most is Sarah to be beside me.

This week was rough. I worked on Sunday night. I got home from work early Monday morning at five o'clock and I had a test in my class at eight. I was going to stay up and go to it then come home after to sleep. I was so hungry that I made some fish when I got home. But I lay down and instantly fell asleep. I didn't wake up until around three in the afternoon, missed my test, and went back to work at five in the afternoon. On Tuesday night I had to go to bed very early because I had to wake up for work at five o'clock.

I missed Sarah a lot but we hadn't been sending messages to

each other very much. I picked up the phone and was going to send her a message just to tell her that I missed her or that I was going to bed early. I didn't know what to say. Whatever I wanted to say just seemed so irrelevant. About two minutes after I put the phone down, Sarah sent me a message. I was so relieved and felt so good, I fell asleep immediately after reading it.

I was at work and the longing for Sarah's company has caused me to shed light on the situation with the women I work with, if it *is* light. My whole spirit is wounded, frostbitten and mending in my bedroom. My spirit should be out on the streets where it shines under the hot sun, able to rehearse my thoughts and go on clearly without the snowy clutter discouraging everything I ache and urge to do. I was counting the nail polish beside one of the women I work with. "I want to buy a girl a gift, and every time I see a nice shirt, or nice pants, or a nice dress at work, I want to buy it for a girl," I began telling her. I have the urge to buy Sarah something. I then told the woman I work with that I broke a woman's dress. She asked how. "We were having fun," I said. "Ew!" she replied.

That was the night after Sarah and I first performed at the college. Sarah took me off to a gazebo in the college courtyard and surprised me, getting on top of me and kissing me furiously. The straps of her dress broke off. I told my coworker about the next time Sarah came over after that night. I was worried that I ruined her dress so I asked her what size she wears. "Why? Are you going to buy me a dress?" Sarah asked me. "I'm not buying you a fucking dress!" I replied.

Thinking about it, I should have bought her a dress. Stephanie, another girl I work with, overheard the conversation about 'having fun' and the broken dress. Later that night, I looked straight into Stephanie's eyes. "It hasn't been good lately," I admitted to her. She had been on the bus with me before work, and told me about a couple people in her life who had died recently.

When we got off the bus, she pointed out the moon. "It's a Cheshire smile," she said. "What?" I asked. She explained that the upside down sliver of the moon looked like a smiling mouth and the term for it was a Cheshire smile.

After work, both of us were tired. Standing, waiting to leave work, Stephanie stood in front of me and started crying. I asked her if something was wrong or if she was just tired. She told me she was just tired. Regardless, it was the very reciprocal of what I had been feeling since Sarah had stopped working just before Christmas.

About an hour after midnight, when it became Valentine's Day I sent Stephanie a text message. I felt bad, I kind of like her. She is very dark and mysterious in many ways. I don't feel the same as my wandering soul did with Victoria. I love Sarah Benton. I wish for her to tell me I have to look for no one other than her but my desire to lie beside a woman, be loved by a woman, and the absence of all of that has caused me to wander a little bit and see what else there is. Stephanie responded in the afternoon on Valentine's Day. My feelings had dissipated since midnight so I just told her I was glad to have her number.

I really thought that if I got a job and I could pay for the wine and Thai food, or pizza and beer, it would make Sarah happy. I thought it would make things easier for her if I wasn't asking her to support me all the time. Instead, I started working and all that has happened is she's been distant. She favours her other friends over me. I see her at school and I send her messages. Her interest seems to be waning.

Sarah says she's going to see me during the spring break. The weather in February is not very nice. I have had an imprisoned spirit stuck in from the cold for some time now. The only solace I have had since I started working is the turntable I bought with my first pay check. It cost me a hundred dollars. I had about fifty vinyl records which I have been collecting since I was eighteen years old. I went to my parents' house and gathered some of the old records they had collected many years ago. I also bought five new ones from the vinyl record store downtown including the Bob Dylan record.

My favourite one so far has been Leonard Cohen, *Songs from a Room*. I listened to it three times last night. It reminded me of Alaina. She used to fall asleep talking to me on the phone like my sister did. Perhaps if I don't see Sarah, I should call her instead. I never talk to her on the phone. I used to spend hours on the phone with girls when I was in my teens and early twenties. I'm not sure why that stopped. I guess everyone got jobs or got married or had kids. Sarah is twenty-one years old. She doesn't have to worry about that happening to her for quite some time. Still, being thirty-two years old is proving to be a much better time in my life than my twenties ever was.

I'm almost graduated from college, I fell in love for the first time since I was twenty-one and I have the highest paying job I've ever had. If only I could do something about my anxiety. I remember what Anaïs Nin said about love and anxiety. She said, when you try to ask someone else for help, they end up scared and backing off because they don't want to get pulled into the deep end with you, to paraphrase. Sarah has said the same thing to me once. I don't think she's ever even read Anaïs Nin but sometimes Sarah is brilliant and sometimes Sarah surprises me. Maybe things will turn around.

# Chapter Ten

*Monday, March 9, 2015*

The window has been open for about an hour. The temperature in here is nice, like a well air conditioned house in the summer. Yesterday the sun was shining, the walk I had was perfect and I was looking forward to the extra hour of daylight at night. I sat at my new favourite spot, the park with the houses all surrounding it. It was still covered by a foot and a half of densely packed snow but the bench was clear and dry. I sat on it and listened to music through my earphones. I came home and it was time for church. I was supposed to work in the morning but I set my alarm clock improperly and I slept in.

When I went to see the psychiatrist at the end of February, my doctor wasn't there but I told the nurse about my new job and the pitiful work hours it was affording me. She suggested I quit and look for something else. Last week, I had to work until ten in the evening and I didn't get home until an hour after that and I was scheduled to work at four o'clock the following morning. I didn't go.

I stayed up and messaged Sarah on my phone until one o'clock in the morning. She's been having a rough time. One of her old boyfriends died a couple of weeks ago. I told her that I really wanted her to be well, and it was okay that she hadn't seen me because I knew it would never be how it was when I fell for her.

I really fell for her in the summer, before I had ever kissed her. The first night she came to my room last spring it was very easy to kiss her. I could have, I should have, but I didn't. She had a boyfriend and my conscience was telling me to lay back. Instead the highlight of that night was dancing with her slow and romantically to the Buddy Holly song *True Love Ways*. In the summer we spent weeks together, every day swimming, laughing, eating at restaurants, drinking, biking, walking, basking in the sunlight, looking after her sister's dog, meeting people in the busy summer streets. It came to an end one night after we danced at the club. "We might as well be dating," she said.

We sat down, she told me she really liked me and said she didn't love me. We left the club and she told me she loved her boyfriend. She took her bike and left without me. I sat there by myself for a few minutes, took my bike and chased after her. When I caught up, she said, "I don't want to talk to you right now."

In those few weeks we were becoming close but two weeks later she also kissed my next door neighbour, Eric. It was a harsh end to the best thing I had ever experienced in my life.

When I missed that first shift, my boss sent me an e-mail saying that if I missed two more, I would be terminated. I wasn't going to be able to make it to church that day because of work. I went for a walk when I missed work because I was surprised by the nice weather. I got back home in time to leave for church but I didn't go because I hadn't had a shower in two days. I had just seen Sarah on Friday. I took a shower and shaved for her on Friday too. It was the first time I had seen her in over a month. When I went for a walk, the first song I played was the song that I played when I woke up beside Sarah for the first time. I specifically loaded it on my phone to listen to it while I walked that morning. It made me cry when I woke up beside Sarah and it made me cry again yesterday.

I sent Sarah a message Sunday afternoon that I had the movie we discussed when she was here and we could watch it sometime soon. She didn't send me a reply for several hours. I was already looking forward to the next time I would see her and her taciturnity made me uneasy, especially with job loss a hop, skip and a jump away. Around seven o'clock she told me she wanted to come over and watch *A Hard Days' Night*.

The whole time Sarah was here visiting, the window was open and I noted how the temperature was still nice inside. After the movie, she played the Buddy Holly song *True Love Ways* and we danced to it a second time. "We always dance to this song," she said. It was slow and awkward touching her close for the first time in about three months. She drank wine, I made lasagna, and when we were tired, I closed the window and we slept beside one another again. I went to my class at eight in the morning and when I got home from class she was gone.

I have to work tomorrow night until early Wednesday morning and then again at dawn the next morning. I'm going to have to go to those shifts no matter how difficult it is, no matter how much the nurse says it's detrimental to my health. No matter what, I can't lose that job. If I don't have that job, I won't be able to do fun things with Sarah like we did when she was working and I had no job. I've tried to create a kind of balance between

Sarah and I and it seems that by working it's a little easier and that might allow me to pick our love up from the depths.

I think for the past two months I haven't been worried about the future. I admit, I wondered if Sarah would come back. But living with an income has afforded me all the provisions I've needed. The things I wanted to do when I was unemployed have become available to me and the confidence it gives me in my future has returned.

A few times I've told Sarah I didn't know what I was going to do with my life. That's what's different when you're twenty. You don't look down on your life, you live knowing the potential. At least I did. I don't know if some people see their potential, but really, when you're young, your potential is almost unlimited. I love that about Sarah. I don't know what she's going to do later but it's likely to be good.

When you don't think about the future, you tend to focus on the either the past or the present. I admit, I did think about Sarah and I, and what we accomplished together over the past year before she came back yesterday. I looked back at the two-hundred-or-so letters I had from Nina. It made me sick to read them. I don't know why I wasted my life when I had so much potential.

But ultimately, the need for enjoyment in the present was calling with the most alarming ring I've heard in nearly fifteen years. When I'm with Sarah Benton, there's no present I could imagine being better, although things have been better.

When you have nothing left to focus on, only the present, the present eventually fails to satisfy. She brought a cup with her for the wine last night. It was given to her at Christmas from one of her classmates. I still haven't given anything to her that resembles a gift. She has one of my shirts that she says she wears to sleep. She told me it looked nice and I told her she should have it because it didn't fit me right. It's hers now. And I think that someday I'd like to give her something meaningful. My time is what I focus on giving her. I look forward to April coming. I met Sarah at the beginning of April. I want to see her this year, on that day, at the same place where we met. Without balking, I could tell her I love her again.

But knowing the danger of losing my job is possible, and knowing that the future, and moreover, the near future is slightly more uncertain again, my need to get higher tonight or any other night has been subdued for focus on necessity and future goals. It feels relieving—it feels like where I was around Christmas when I got the job, but with better weather. Everything is better when the weather is nice. I've never known what life is like with too much of anything—too much love, or too much money. I've had too much food and that doesn't help or feel good. I'm glad Sarah hasn't given me too much and I'm glad I don't have too much, because I'd probably blunder all my gains and donate what's left to some poor girl. She can have me now because right now I think I'm good for her, although things have been worse.

# Chapter Eleven

*Monday, April 27, 2015*

I've been longboarding a lot lately. Sarah has started learning guitar and I'm showing her how to play various things. She's helping me gain more confidence on the longboard. She used to skateboard as a young girl and says she was fairly proficient at it. I remember in the fall, we watched *Chitty Chitty Bang Bang* and she longboarded to the movie rental store while I biked. She was very fast. I had a longboard last year but I fell off going down a hill and scraped my knee and elbows and ripped my brand new jeans. I was kind of intimidated by it after that.

I usually walk but since I've been longboarding, walking has been taking a back seat. It's a lot faster to longboard around. I can't really think much when I longboard, it's mostly an adrenaline rush and it has prevented me from rehearsing my thoughts. Not to mention the end of the semester got kind of hectic and I've spent more time with Sarah in the past two weeks than I did in December, January, February and March, combined. She says we're going to go swimming a lot in the summer and she's going to come play guitar with me too.

It seems like everything is going faster these days. It's fun to get the ball rolling and watch everything start up again but what happens when the ball is going too fast? It's difficult for me to process everything that's going on now. I get together with Sarah and for the most part I really have no intentions other than to make her laugh, see if she'll kiss me again and make her feel something deep. I can't really think fast enough to make that happen most times—or things are going too fast for me to be able to think of something.

I did tell her I really like her legs. She thinks her legs aren't beautiful. It's strange because it's probably her legs that I find most beautiful, aside from her pretty face. She has beautiful golden coloured eyes.

I've been buying a lot of wine for her because her work savings has dwindled down to nothing, and aside from the food and shelter her parents are providing, she's living off of a government tax credit that comes once a month. For me, that check would last about a week, just buying stuff at Tim Horton's. For her it probably goes into a couple nights of drinking. I also paid for a couple of concert tickets for a show we're going to see in Toronto after her final semester is over. We're going to rent out a dorm at the University of Toronto and spend the night together there. I'm very much looking forward to that.

But Sarah recently reminded me of when she had money and I always told her I'd pay her back for the beer and wine she bought. I always paid her back but when I did she always put the money towards more beer or more wine to drink with me. I remember her generosity. Now it's my turn. I always thought I was tonight but if there's anyone who's tonight, it's Sarah. She lives for the high, getting higher and higher and has little regard for how she's going to come down. At least with me she's like that. I've come to realize that I'm not tonight anymore, I'm tomorrow. I have pretty close to everything I want, and it's all given to me worry free.

I'm not sure when or how I changed but somewhere along the way I became less concerned about taking the night to the extreme or living purely for the moment. I suspect that the more frequently you get to that extreme pleasure threshold, the less worried you become about reaching it. In the case of Sarah, I suspect that she doesn't realize it yet but there's no place higher for her to reach until someday danger takes over her journeys and reasonability sets in, like me crashing my car ten years ago. I think she admires tomorrow. I think I'm the most reliable and responsible person she's ever been with but maybe it is Sarah's way of getting higher that makes me look so reasonable.

She's not *always* pushing the boundaries of pleasure. I think she wanted to feel sad a couple days ago. It's something I do as well. She was playing music that reminded her of the past. On top of that, one of her old boyfriends died recently and I suspect the thought of him gone makes her terribly sad. So she sat on my bed crying and listening to the songs that would coax her to cry. Whatever it was, it was her being tonight. I want to show her that she has everything and that there is much more to life than just tonight. There's more to being with me than just tonight. Maybe one day she will find it and maybe it'll bring her close to me again.

I was worried for a while that I'd have to wait thirteen years to be with a woman again, that unlucky number. I told a friend from work, who was feeling depressed, that something always happens to change your mind about feeling sad. I told her it's not immediate or exactly what you want but something always happens to change the sadness you have into happiness or at least neutrality.

I put down the phone and went in and shaved the hair on my crotch, hoping that I'd be with a woman again. Sarah came over that night. We played guitar and listened to music. I never want her to leave me when she leaves. After she left, Anna came over unexpectedly and we had sex and she slept with me again. I can't decide if I was happy or just neutral.

At the end of the week, I had a great conversation with my sister. She told me my dad says "he'll come around one day." I guess I'm regarded by my family as lost somewhere. My sister says I was quite advanced socially as a child. She says now I need to get a grip on my emotions. She told me about her past life. She was a textile trader in Montreal in one past life. She says she did well as a textile trader because she could get along well with a lot of people. She mentioned that my grandmother used to work in a textile factory in Saltaire, England when our father was a baby. She was giving me a ride downtown and when we got there we just continued our conversation, parked in her car for almost an hour.

She asked me if I thought of myself as a spiritual medium and she advised me to stay away from evil spirits. She also told me not to mention any of our conversation to anyone because people think that people who talk about spirits and past lives are crazy. I don't—I talked to Sarah about past lives about a week later. I told my sister that I had one experience taking mushrooms with Shawn, on the banks of Lake Ontario, that I felt like I witnessed my death in a previous life. I felt as though, in a past life, I was somewhat of a bad man, evil perhaps, who got murdered as a consequence. I also told Sarah about the same thing and she said she believes our purpose is the same in both past and present lives. At one time, Sarah was a wood nymph.

It's strange that despite everything I have and cherish in my present life, the only thing I'd give it up for is to go out into the woods and live with nature. I'd do that and I think I'd be happy doing it. I really want to. Sarah really liked the Ayn Rand book *Anthem*. I read it and the moment where the main character breaks free of civilization and finds a home alone in the woods, freer than anyone had thought possible, seemed like it captured my dream. Sarah tells me I should go after it and live my dreams. If there ever was one, that would be it. It could include her. Her purpose in this life is the same. She'd move out to the woods with me and we'd live off the fat of the land like they tried to in *Of Mice and Men*.

Speaking of which, sometimes I feel like squeezing Sarah to death because I love her so much. Maybe some things didn't really need a disclaimer. Some things were about right.

The sad part is, before you know it, tonight's over, you're waiting for tomorrow and suddenly it's today again. Sarah seems to be able to act and respond as fast as her heart is beating in every situation, which explains why she used to be an actress in high school. But perhaps I'm not slow. "He'll come around one day," is the phrasing my father supposedly used. Perhaps I'm just waiting for my time like my dad says, when really, tomorrow never does arrive. It seems like it would be a little cliché for a musician to be always on time.

So, where do I get off the train if it's only theoretical for me to arrive? One day I'll come around—in the forest, maybe in a graduation ceremony, maybe in a line up at the Sally Anne, maybe in a plane crash.

I think I feel elated.

# Chapter Twelve

*Friday, May 8, 2015*

Sarah is planting trees in some Ontario wetland today. We spoke on the phone last night. We plan to do another performance soon and start working on some new material but she's unable to see me for the weekend. This summer, she'll be building a system to collect water to study the composition of the water she finds. It's for her final graduation report in her college program where she learns about the science of the environment.

She participated in a campaign to get an organic waste composting program at the college. For some reason it fell through. I told her the college probably contracts a company to do the waste removal and that she really would have to deal with them and not the college.

She'll probably make an excuse to see me at some point and it'll be fine. She'll probably want to play guitar with me when she takes a break from her schoolwork. She wrote the beginnings of a song recently. It sounds very nice and she wants me to help her with it. When she started playing guitar, I finally played her some of my songs. Her favourite is the catchiest, fastest song I ever wrote. It's about a couple of my friends that I played music with in the past. Sarah always asks me to play that one now. I didn't play her the song about Victoria and Jennifer. I think it's the most depressing song I've ever written.

It helped that I started to write because my thoughts weren't so clear for a while. Most of that first book I wrote was too incomprehensible to be published. By the end of it, the writing became clearer and I was beginning to be healthy in my mind again. I remembered the distinct thought that despite being in love with one woman and wishing to be in a relationship with her, I would never again let my simultaneous opportunities with other women pass me by.

I remember one night I went to see a concert by the Barenaked Ladies with Victoria and Jennifer, in the first couple months of my first year of college. I thought Jennifer was attractive, and we went on a date the week before that. She had tickets to the Toronto International Film Festival and she asked me to go. The movie was a very unusual independent film that probably didn't get released on VHS. DVDs started coming out around that time but it was unusual to meet a poor college student with an expensive DVD player.

After the movie, Jennifer asked me to come back to her place. Deep down, I know that this was more than just an invitation. I think it was really my chance to get close to a woman. I don't think she was interested in a relationship with me but I let chances like that pass me by so many times that I just can't anymore.

She told me she was waiting for a friend to call her so she had to go meet her just after midnight. I suspect that she was letting me have an excuse to leave her after we got physical at her place. For whatever reason, I don't think women understand that men are really not as they are depicted in movies and television. Movies and television tell women men don't want to sleep beside them, that they just want to leave after sex. I don't think she was aware that the most moving experience I had ever had with a woman was just sleeping beside her.

My roommate, Amy, Anna's sister, the girl who drove me into the mental hospital before I met Sarah, was around last weekend. She offered me a beer and we sat on the doorstep drinking a beer and smoking cigarettes. I was waiting for Sarah to come over. After we had a beer, Amy asked me to come back to her room so I asked her if I could have another beer there and she said I could. When we got there, she immediately lay down under the blankets in her bed. She told me to lie down with her. We lay there for a few minutes. My chest was against her back but she was reaching behind to hold on to me. She then got up and turned off the light and came back to bed. She took off her pants and moved my hand over her naked hip. I reached between her legs. I asked her if it felt good. "I want you inside of me," she replied.

I actually like her quite a bit. When I first met her, we spent a lot of time together. I didn't know her very well but I became very attracted to her and got very frustrated with her that she wasn't interested in me as more than just a friend.

I kissed her, told her she was beautiful and left after we made love last weekend. I didn't see her again until Wednesday, two nights ago, after Sam, Sarah, and I came here from Tim Horton's. I asked Amy to watch a movie with me and she told me she would on Thursday night when she got home from work. I went back to my room, then she came a few minutes later and we watched a movie. She had to be up for work before seven in the morning, and she left my room just after midnight. The next day, I went to see her when I got home from work but she was too tired to do anything.

Anna is a crazy alcoholic with a nasty boyfriend, but her sister is beautiful and sweet and attracts me with her calm and subtle personality. Amy talks about how her sister abuses her sweet nature and uses her for a place to stay and to buy alcohol. I believe that she is a good-natured, good-hearted girl, not like her sister, and that we could be happy.

After the Barenaked Ladies concert with Victoria and Jennifer, we walked back to the subway entrance beside the Royal Ontario Museum and both Victoria and Jennifer went to their respective dorms from there. Jennifer gave me her phone number before she left. I walked down the stairs to the subway stop and before I walked through the turnstile, I turned around to chase after Jennifer through the park. I got up the stairs and ran through the park towards where Jennifer pointed out her dorm after our movie date. As I reached The Philosopher's Walk in the University of Toronto campus an old man stopped me from running. Jennifer was nowhere in sight. I guess I was chasing her because I had thought about what I had missed out on after our date the week before.

"Stop! You don't need to go so fast. You have lots of time," the old man said to me. I looked at him speechless. In that very moment, I thought his statement was a bit of a curse but I felt like he was wise and wouldn't say that to hurt me, that he was probably right. I kept walking for a while until the man had left and then I turned around to finally get on the subway.

Sarah never did show up on the night I made love with Amy but I'm going back to Toronto, to a concert and staying at a dorm for the night with Sarah this summer. I think in some way, a little bit of my spirit is still there in Toronto. And more than anything right now, I want Sarah to help me end the philandering by being with me romantically.

There's a certain requirement of patience to move forward with Amy. While at any time with Sarah, I could ask her to be my girlfriend and the timing would seem appropriate. What that wise old man said on The Philosopher's Walk has haunted me for years—with Jennifer, and any of the casual female acquaintances I've had since. I've recounted this in a timely fashion since it would be defiance if I was to pursue Amy in haste.

In many ways, not being with a girl regularly for almost ten years was very essential to me treating Sarah the way that I did. All of the times that I felt like she wanted to be with me and all the times when I felt like I had nothing and that I was nothing more than a drinking buddy to her have meant more to me because I hadn't experienced those feelings in so long. When it feels bad, it's actually good and when it feels good, it's inconceivable. It seems impossible for me to find meaning with anyone else because Sarah opened my heart up again. She expressed interest in me when there was none. She found me lying decrepit in my hole and saved my sorry ass from permanent decay.

It feels wrong to put everything on hold, stop this charging boulder and open up for somebody new. I just wish some wise man would see me with Sarah when I'm in Toronto. "Hurry up! Life is passing you by. There's no time like the present," I wish he'd say.

Before I watched that movie with Amy, Sarah bought me a bagel and a coffee at Tim Horton's. She was drunk and she bought it with cream cheese, not knowing I don't like cream cheese. She got upset that the nice gesture didn't work out as well as she had hoped. Sarah ate the bagel herself. I told her I was sorry and I asked her if she was really upset. "You're in the doghouse," she said jokingly.

# Chapter Thirteen

*Thursday, June 25, 2015*

It's been close to nineteen years since I've had a girlfriend. After we went for coffee and a bagel, we came back to my place, which is just around the corner, and Amy was coming out of the backyard. In that very moment, I felt bad that I could be with her, but wasn't. It was comforting that Sam was there, and Amy didn't see me alone with another girl. Deep down, I felt like she was out there hoping she'd run into me. She did, only I was with Sarah. Amy went back inside, and I became pensive about how it would be nice to see Amy soon. After Sarah left, I ran into Amy again and told her we should watch a movie sometime. I told her we could get some potato chips.

I had plans to go to that open mic church thing again when Sunday came, but I ran into Amy and she asked me if I wanted to drink with her. We started drinking together sometime in the afternoon. I was having a good time so I sent Pastor Derek a message telling him I had a date that night and I couldn't go. We spent about another hour talking in the backyard. Eventually, we went to the porch at the front door and sat there talking. Amy started talking about a past relationship that she had had, and was talking about it as if she was unlucky with relationships. I thought about it and I decided she wouldn't be unlucky for long. I was a little late delivering the question but I did ask her to be my girlfriend and she said she would.

We hadn't talked about the sex we had the week before but immediately after we started going out, she mentioned that we had already had sex. We both agreed that having already had sex together was kind of good. I'm glad we didn't talk about our first encounter before I asked her out because I would have told her that that night I was waiting around for Sarah to come at ten in the evening, but she didn't show up. It was a stroke of luck because if Sarah had come to visit, I would likely be headed towards nineteen years without a girlfriend, heck maybe twenty. With my luck with women, you never know.

The next week, I told Sarah that I was in a relationship. She sent me a message asking me to hang out, but I was lying down with Amy and didn't respond for quite a few hours. Sarah got upset and I broke down and told her about Amy. A couple days after that, I guess it was convenient for Sarah to tell me she was in a relationship with another guy as well. I suppose it wasn't important to tell me this before, but I think her reticence was in fact healthier for me and I may not have ended up with Amy if she had told me.

Aside from my recent influx of sexual desires, and lust for belonging with the opposite sex, I've had my mind on two other things. I started thinking about the first thing before the beginning of my relationship with Amy, and the other started popping into my thoughts mostly after we started going out. The first being the Ernest Hemingway book, *The Old Man and the*

*Sea*, and the second being that strange eighteen years without a girlfriend. I lacked love, and very much needed to replace it with something. I know now what I was giving up and what I was going to replace it with.

The night I was with Sarah and Sam, when Amy came around from the backyard, I didn't stay up very late because the next morning I had to get up at four in the morning to go to work. I woke up for work that morning, and went for a bagel and a coffee at Tim Horton's while I waited for my ride to work. It was about a two hour drive to a small city on Georgian Bay. When I got to the coffee shop, one of my past classmates was in there as well. He was reading a book.

He was a young, Korean immigrant in Canada for college. I think he was about twenty years old. We greeted each other and I sat at the table in front of his because I didn't want to disturb him. We weren't great friends but for some reason we kept talking. I suppose it was a little unusual to both be in a Tim Horton's at four-thirty in the morning. He was waiting to take the bus to go home to Toronto. I asked him what book he was reading. I couldn't tell what it was called because it was in Korean. "The Old Man in the Sea, have you heard of it?" he answered. "Oh yeah, Hemingway, right?" I said.

We had worked together on a project for nearly three months in the school term that had just ended and one of our partners talked about his obsession with women and lovers more than I do. It got to the point where I was a little upset that we were talking about blowjobs and testicular licking a little too much for my liking. Our Korean partner mainly talked about marriage. He mentioned marriage again as we sat in Tim Horton's. He asked me to move to his table. We talked about women. I told him I hadn't had a girlfriend in eighteen years. He noted that I was fourteen when I last had a girlfriend. I did have in the back of my mind that I had had sex with Amy less than a week before that.

But for some reason, I think because it was in Korean and I was worried about the second thing that had been on my mind, I found *The Old Man and the Sea* to be a bit of a coincidental title for me at the time. Being alone for eighteen years makes you feel a little like an old man in a relationship with the sea. I've never read the book, so I don't really know what it's about, but since then I looked everywhere in town for that book to try to read it. It's a mere hundred pages, more or less. I could read it in just an afternoon.

I was early for work the last time I went about looking for it, about a month ago now. I was three hours early, to be exact. I ran into Sam and his girlfriend Shanna, Sarah's friends, while waiting for my shift to start. Sam was headed to buy some beer and he suggested I go see the newest movie playing at the theatre down the road, to kill some time. I decided I would go that way but I ended up at the used book store instead. Looking back on that day, it was meant to be coincidental to me, no matter how I was to have sliced it. If I went to the movie, I would have ran into one of my friends, whom I found out was also there, but something very interesting also happened at the bookstore, which is also making me think about that second thing which has been popping into my mind.

I gave up a little bit of myself in those early years, with that first girlfriend of mine. In some ways, I was the happiest I've ever been. It was like I completed a puzzle and I looked at it and I was proud to have completed it. It lasted about eight weeks. We met on Fridays and some Saturdays. But in the couple of years after she broke it off with me, it felt as though she had stolen a couple of the pieces to that puzzle and looking at the remaining puzzle always reminded me of that happy feeling, but also how it had all been ruined at her mercy.

At the same time, while my pride was high, I picked up a love for jazz music. I learned to play jazz music really well. I attribute it to visiting a pizza shop in the city where there was live jazz music every Friday—the same night of the week we used to have our dates together. I was moved by the performances of one guitar player in the band. He was the youngest one in the group.

Because of those early moments, I have an odd connection between pizza and jazz music. Sometimes when I hear jazz music, I crave pizza and when I eat pizza I desire to hear jazz music. Because I was in the diminishing wake of my soul's feeling complete, this connection came about between pizza and jazz in some strange Pavlovian way.

I replaced love with jazz and pizza and now, in a way, you could say it's returned to an obsession for love. I've had pizza and jazz connected in my mind for nearly twenty years, or for as long as I've lacked having a girlfriend. I stopped performing jazz music about two years ago. I haven't played jazz music anywhere since I've been living here in the same house as Amy. In fact, I think my goal of trying to find a woman has occupied my mind so much that I haven't had time to really play much jazz.

With Sarah it was pop music, or some slightly sub pop genre that we ascribed to liking. I've really had to shelf jazz music aside to attract women in the past and now as well. Women tend not to like jazz music very much and if they say they like jazz, it usually means they don't hate it and won't turn it off immediately.

As I looked for *The Old Man and the Sea* in that used bookstore, a young woman entered the bookstore and asked the shop owner if he had any jazz instruction books. I thought it over, dozens of times, wondering if I should mention that I had piles of jazz instruction books she could buy. I could meet this woman, who was interested in my favourite music, but I thought of Amy. I let her look at the ridiculous selection of books the shop owner suggested, thinking still of my girlfriend and I let her walk out of the store without saying a word about my horde of jazz books. I think deep down I actually miss playing jazz music.

I didn't find the book I was looking for either. I did however find a copy of *Love in the Time of Cholera*. The novel sounded romantic when I read the back of the book. It's the story of a man who loves a young woman but she marries a wealthy doctor. He loves her so much that, despite being sexual with several women, he reserves his love for her until her husband dies and they're both elderly.

I couldn't afford it though, so I left with nothing and went to work. It was fifteen dollars and I only had eighteen. After work, I met Amy at her work and we walked home together. I fell asleep in her arms that night. She didn't spend the night with me but her presence seemed to relax my nerves.

I would say that I've found those pieces, gotten those bits back from that first girlfriend. It's not because of Amy—it's not because of anything. It's not because my first girlfriend is married now and has a respectable job as a school teacher and went to law school. I don't know why everything changed for me lately, but my soul still doesn't feel satisfied the way I did that first time I had a girlfriend. I think in those eighteen years, I came to realize that it was so insignificant to reclaim any of those missing bits because I had become a much better person for having once lost some of it.

I have to admit, however significant or insignificant Amy may or may not be to me now, I'm very glad I gave up pizza. I had to replace pizza and jazz with something, and if you had to choose between love, sex, pizza and jazz, I'm sure you'd decide the way I did.

I think there is something missing still, though, because I came to love being by myself for so long, having freedom to do whatever I wanted, with whomever I wanted, with men or women, and now I can't. I can sneak around and do things behind Amy's back like an episode of *Mad Men* but I can't really reclaim the feeling of truly being free. I guess it was the same when I was a jazz musician. You get known for jazz and then nobody thinks of you when they want their new band to sound like Arctic Monkeys.

I guess what Nina wrote to me in her letters was true: "Life is a game of bait and switch." When I read that for the first time it really hit me hard, and the lessons I gained from her were some of the hardest ones I've ever tried to grasp. I think partly because most of our relationship was on paper and you can be quite bleak, deep and stark when you're afforded the thoughtful nature of the written word.

It might seem early to do so but I've been looking at one-bedroom apartments with Amy this past week. We've been together just over a month and we already intend to live together in an apartment. It is, however, like a television drama the way I go about seeing Sarah now. I told Amy I was at my parents' house for Father's Day the last time I was with Sarah.

Sarah and I walked downtown to go to an underground-experimental-pop show, drinking vodka and peach juice. I got back just after ten in the evening and Amy suspected nothing. Sarah comes over, stays for a while and we have a great time, she leaves, then shortly after, Amy returns from work. Sarah's presence points out to me everything I miss about being single.

In light of the remaining feelings I have for Sarah Benton, I intend to read *Love in the Time of Cholera*. It came in the mail this morning while I was out for a walk. It's been on my bed all day.

The weather has been satisfyingly warm and it's hard to stay indoors. I think I'm going to revive my time as The Buddha and read it under a tree in the park behind the house I live in with Amy. Or maybe I'll go to that new spot with the houses all surrounding the park, that I saw when my shadow crept up and scared me. I still haven't yet had much use for that spot. Sarah wants to go swimming with me again this summer. I want to as well.

# Chapter Fourteen

*Monday, July 6, 2015*

A week after the underground experimental-pop show, Sarah brought me down to the lakeside spot where she spent Canada Day with her boyfriend and her best friend. I stayed in, watched movies, and had sex with Amy on Canada Day. I met Sarah at a park on her way to the lake front. When she got there, she had a jug full of vodka and juice. We drank it as we walked. I told her I was hungry and we had to stop for some food at some point. It was amicable and she told me about some situation with her boyfriend and I talked about my situation with Amy.

Amy claims she's an Oscar winner, Ben Affleck is her cousin, she was friends with the late actor Heath Ledger, she was engaged to Jack White from The White Stripes and that he stabbed her in the stomach. She also claims she was once a Playboy Playmate, was a General in the army, got hit by a missile, and had a baby that her sister killed. Oh, and she also published a book of poetry that sold less than fifty copies. She's a pathological liar. She lies for no reason whatsoever. Even Anna told me the Playboy and missile things were fabrications. I can't figure out why she does it but it makes anything she tells me about her past very difficult to believe.

So as we were going to the lake front, Sarah and I decided to go to the liquor store to replenish our alcohol supply. As we made our way there, we ran into Sarah's friends, Sam and Shanna. I said that I had to leave before ten, so I could be home when Amy got home from work. Sarah made plans to meet up with her friends after. As we approached the liquor store, Sarah told me she had taken up tennis with her boyfriend. "Why did you do that?" I asked.

"I've always wanted to play tennis," she said.

"You told me you didn't like tennis when I asked you to play with me." I responded. I was quite upset that she wouldn't play tennis with me but she would for her boyfriend. She didn't seem to remember telling me a year ago that she didn't like tennis.

We both bought three large cans of beer and stuffed them into Sarah's bag while standing in the liquor store parking lot. After that we walked down the main drag and found a sandwich restaurant. Sarah didn't want anything but was enticed to have something when we got there. She mentioned that she watched the Woody Allen movie, *Annie Hall*, again. She did her almost dead on, Annie Hall impression and stated her love for Diane Keaton in that movie. I had given her a copy of it around the same time as I asked her to play tennis with me last year. I thought she would really like it. "You watched it again?" I asked.

"Yeah, I love that movie, don't you?" She then began to list off some of her favourite parts from the movie.

"I don't really remember it very well, but I know I liked it." I told her.

"And Diane Keaton is so hot in that movie."

"I guess." I really did think Diane Keaton was very sexy in that movie (and I thought partially that Sarah would identify with Annie Hall's fashion sense, which she did because she now has a hat that she has called the Annie Hall hat) but that wasn't why I liked that movie. I saw it when I was about sixteen years old. Diane Keaton's character was quite possibly more than twice my age when I saw that movie.

"I wonder how Woody Allen landed a girl like that," she mentioned.

I may have said "yeah," in response.

I'm not sure exactly what I said, but I know in real life they weren't in a relationship, so what the actors looked like wasn't terribly important to me, but I didn't say that either.

"But, I guess comedians are very confident," she remarked. It hit me hard that she said that. For one thing, you have to be remarkably good-looking to have a good-looking girlfriend or else you have to be extremely confident. It felt like she was knocking me for being so insecure all the time. On top of my insecurities, her boyfriend is notably more attractive than I am.

We finished our sandwiches and began walking to her lakeside spot. I didn't say anything. I had become insulted, and extremely pouty. Just before we got to her spot (which was perfectly secluded for drinking), she told me, "Stop being so lame!" I couldn't snap out of it.

This is how she has always insulted me. She complimented me on my shirt when we met in the park, complimented my new bracelet as we walked to the liquor store, but she took it all back and stomped on me too.

I just sat there drinking on the lake with her, speaking only when I absolutely needed to. She just played guitar, and I stared out onto the lake thinking I wasn't good enough for her and that's why she went out with someone else. I cried a little bit and I wiped my tears. By the time we had finished two beers her friends had begun to text her to meet up. She told me I didn't have to stay. I couldn't tell if she meant I should leave because I was being pouty or because she knew I had to get back before Amy got home from work.

I liked her friends that she was meeting up with. By the time ten o'clock came around, Amy was messaging me telling me she was on her way home. It was the first time I admitted I was out with Sarah. She didn't seem to mind too much. It was the first time I had spent any time with Shanna, but I had spent time with Sam the day Sarah bought me the bagel with cream cheese. He was also the one who suggested I go see that movie, the night I had the opportunity to meet the young lady looking for jazz instruction books.

Shanna and Sarah were on the swings in the park where we went to meet them and I was talking to Sam about Sarah insulting me. I told him I was being pouty and he mentioned that his girlfriend does just the same thing to him. It made me feel a little better. Sam had a can of beer and a flask with a bit of rum. We ran out of liquor soon after we met so we took a cab back to Shanna and Sam's place where they had a case of beer and half a bottle of rum waiting. Sam and I had both received our work payments that day.

Sam has a famous quote from *Fear and Loathing in Las Vegas* tattooed on his leg so I showed him a picture I took of a section of a 1970s Rolling Stone magazine I own. The section was written by a reader of the magazine and was about classic Hunter S. Thompson buffoonery. Sam thought it was quite neat. When we got back to their place, which was conveniently close to my place as well as Sarah's, we took shots from the rum and smoked cigarettes. When we got into the case of beer, we started playing a drinking game. Sam's company made me feel great that night. He was like the brother you always wished you had. Shanna and Sam are wonderful together.

We all were a little too drunk, but for some reason (I think Sam drinks a lot of alcohol), Shanna and Sam didn't seem very drunk. I played everyone Leonard Cohen's *Famous Blue Raincoat*, singing, and playing drunkenly on Sarah's guitar. They weren't really paying attention. Sarah and Shanna were making silly videos with their phones and Sam was laughing at them. I don't think Shanna really drank very much at all that night. She seemed kind of upset, and it was none of my business to know why so I didn't ask her about it.

Sarah and I got a little too drunk though. By the time we all were too tired to keep the party going, Shanna and Sam suggested we walk Sarah home, so we started walking Sarah back. Shanna and Sam had kind of left Sarah and me to walk together. When we got to the place where Sarah normally would cut through the park to her house, leaving me to head back farther down the same street, Sarah stopped to say goodbye to me. "Sarah, I love you," I said, before she left.

She came closer to me and told me to kiss her on the cheek. So, I grabbed her and kissed her on the cheek. For some reason, I didn't let her go. We stumbled on the sidewalk, and over the curb, laughing, holding each other in a long hug. Then I kissed Sarah on the mouth. I walked home after that.

I don't remember much about what happened when I got home but I woke up in Amy's bed after she had already left for work in the morning. When Amy got home from work that day, she said I had been very drunk and she tried talking to me but the most I was capable of doing was nodding and shaking my head. She said we had had a few cigarettes on the step, but I don't know if she got it out of me that I made a drunken pass at Sarah just before I came home.

# Chapter Fifteen

*Wednesday, July 29, 2015*

Most of the time, we would just lie on my bed and hold one another. I've become quite lazy because of this inactivity. Sometimes we would watch TV and other times we would listen to music but we hardly ever talked. Sometimes we would drink beer together and Amy would tell me about her delusional episodes that likely never even happened. It made it more difficult to believe any of the stories that were potentially real. She told me she had to abort a pregnancy she had had when she was younger. I didn't know whether I should feel sympathy for her because I couldn't tell if she was being honest or not.

I suppose I should feel sympathy for her that she has delusions and I have had delusions at one time in my life as well. The thing is: I knew my delusions were delusional and I worked toward making myself sane again. She's amazed by her delusions and they give her a sense of self-importance. Besides, she chose to be a Playboy model and fuck rock stars in her delusions. I chose to see God, that great chicken wing. I'm not saying I'm better than her but there's something to be said about the beauty of honesty. Human imagination is an incredible thing but honesty is no mistress.

She can't cook very well. Most of her work money goes to rent and eating out. Most of the time she's too lazy to go to the grocery store to buy food, and I guess when you don't know how to cook food, you don't really want to buy anything at the grocery store. One time I saw her make spaghetti. She put the spaghetti in a plastic container filled with water, put the cover on the container and stuck it in the microwave until it heated up. Then she just emptied some of the water and poured pasta sauce over the wet spaghetti in the container. It was soppy tomato sauce with spaghetti noodles. I don't know how anyone would want to eat that. Most of the time she had no food and I had to make her my food because I didn't want her to spend her money on an over-priced sandwich from one of the restaurants on the corner. She makes more money than me but I always end up having more money than her at the next pay period.

She's so lazy that she never walks anywhere, won't take the bus, and barely knows how to use the bus system. She takes the wrong bus to work every day, choosing to walk an extra half an hour, whether it's raining or hailing. She doesn't want to go on the right bus at a stop that isn't even farther away because it's new and she's used to always going on the wrong bus.

She's been leaving for work in the morning two hours before her shift starts because it takes her so long to get to work and then she complains that she has to get up so early for work. I've told her a handful of times that she's taking the wrong bus every time but she doesn't seem to care. She's the most inept person I've met in my life.

I've had long conversations with Sarah about Amy regarding

these issues. Last year, I gained so much strength in my body because I spent so much time trekking the city on my bike with Sarah. I used to leave Amy sometimes, telling her I had too much energy and I couldn't lie around all day. She'd say she wanted to come for a walk with me and we'd go for a walk. "How long do you walk for?" she'd ask me only about five minutes into our walk. She would already be tired. She couldn't even make it as far as the corner where all the restaurants and stores are. I should have known she couldn't walk for more than five minutes because she always asks me to get coffee for her at Tim Horton's and when she runs out of cigarettes, she won't go buy more, she just smokes mine. Sarah and I were convinced I should break up with her. My apprehension to do so was caused by the feeling that I would probably never have a girlfriend ever again. Sarah, on the other hand is my nearest friend, loves me to a certain extent and convinced me that I have a lot of potential and I would meet somebody else.

I guess it was a couple weeks ago that I met Michelle. I went to class in the morning like every other Tuesday this summer. I had to present a marketing strategy I had come up with for a company. The thing about taking marketing in college is that you meet a lot of very persuasive people who have a lot of talent for selling and pitching things to you.

One of the presentations for Steamwhistle beer was the reason why I met Michelle. It was Amy's day off and it was expected that I would buy us some beer after class. Usually I buy the cheapest beer that they have, so that I can save a bit of money. After seeing my classmates' presentation, though, I really wanted to buy some Steamwhistle. I saw it at the liquor store, I was tempted to buy it, and I did.

As I was walking out of the liquor store, I noticed that there was a free gift in the box of beer I had just bought—a bottle opener. I always carried a bottle opener on my key chain for situations where someone needed a beer opened.

About nine years ago, before I moved here, I was playing a jazz gig every Sunday at a bar in my hometown. Two girls I had known in high school had a few beers they had snuck in to the bar so they didn't have to spend expensive bar prices but they had no bottle opener to open the beers. So they asked me if I could open them, and I told them I could do it without a bottle opener. I took the beers and jimmied the bottles on the edge of the table. It was taking quite long because the table was a little wobbly. Since it was taking so long, the waitress at the bar noticed me opening the beers from the other end of the bar. She came over and the three of us got thrown out, and I got banned from going to the bar, including my gigs, for a month. Ever since, I've always carried a bottle opener with me.

Right after I left the liquor store with the beer, as I was walking to the bus station to head home, I noticed a woman standing away from the bus platform smoking a cigarette. She was listening to music on her earphones. I stopped there too, to have a cigarette. I was trying to look at her face to see what she looked like because she was tall and skinny and looked rather nice. I wanted to see if she had a pretty face. We made eye contact as I was beginning to open my box of beer to get the bottle opener out. I suppose that when I looked at her it may have seemed like I wanted to talk to her so she took her earphones off. "I guess I should be more social eh?" she said. I just shrugged my shoulders like I had no expectations. "I guess," I responded.

I told her that I was happy that I had just got a new bottle opener in my box of beer and that I was going to replace my old bottle opener. I took out my keys and she saw the old bottle opener and she saw the new one. "Is that a guitar?" she asked. The old bottle opener was blue and was shaped like a guitar. "Do you play guitar?" she asked. "I have a bunch of guitars at my place that I never play," she continued. I told her I used to play jazz gigs around town and that I've been in a couple jazz bands before and I asked her why she never plays her guitars. I asked her if they were her boyfriend's guitars. She said they were her guitars, and she thought the old key chain looked nicer.

"I like *this* one better," I said, and I asked her if she wanted to keep the old one. She did. She took the bottle opener and quickly put it on her keychain as I strung the new bottle opener to mine. It was raining lightly that morning, and she told me about her sons and that she was on her way back from her job as a massage therapist. She had a bag full of linens with her, from work.

Because it was raining, I didn't want to stand out there too long, and Amy was expecting me home soon with the beer. I saw my bus coming so I told Michelle I had to go. "Are you on the social network?" she asked, as I was bending over to pick up my beer. "Yes I am, add me!" I responded. As I was walking to my bus I shouted back at her, over the sounds of the loud parked buses. "Maybe we can hang out sometime! Enjoy the rain!"

I came back home and spent the rest of the day lying around drinking beer with Amy but I was thinking about sending Michelle a message. I was dying to talk to her again. I didn't though and got kind of drunk instead. Amy was pleased that I bought more expensive beer and we made love in the afternoon and laughed listening to *Afternoon Delight* by Starland Vocal Band. I waited until the next day to send a message to Michelle.

I was supposed to go to a show downtown with Sarah on Thursday so I invited Michelle to come too. Sarah was going to the underground-rock show with her boyfriend and it would have been the first time I met him. I've seen him a few times with her at school but we've never talked before. Michelle said she had to work a full day on Thursday. When I met her, she said she had to work only a half day. That's why she was going home so early. She said she'd be tired but I should ask her again Thursday when she was done work.

On Thursday when I talked to her, she said she already had plans that she forgot about, with her girlfriend, but she invited me to come. It was an open mic at the community center downtown. I went and we enjoyed the music. After the show, her friend left us alone together and we walked along the main drag downtown, and along the waterfront. She told me about her work, her sons, and some of her friends. One of Michelle's friends was all alone in her house to herself for the weekend because her husband and son were away at camp. She was drinking alone. She came to pick Michelle up downtown around ten o'clock that night so Michelle could stop her slightly alcoholic friend from drinking so much. I went home at that time and arrived just before Amy got home from work.

That weekend I spent Friday and Saturday with Michelle too. There was a concert and beer festival downtown in the park. I really hadn't had that much fun since last Canada Day when I spent the whole week with Sarah.

I remember when I was in grades four to eight I had begun having some amazing summers. I remember that first summer after grade four I met a bunch of new neighbourhood kids and played all-night hide-and-seek, street hockey, baseball, and basketball with them. When I went back to school at the beginning of grade five I remember thinking, "I don't know how I could ever have a better summer than that. That was the best summer I've ever had."

When summer came, after grade five, I again had so much fun, not knowing how I'd ever top the summer I had the year before. For whatever reason, by the time I was heading into grade six, I had had an even better summer than the one before. By the time I was going into grade eight, there were girls, and girlfriends, and kissing and touching legs and so it went that each successive summer after grade four got better than the last.

I don't know when that stopped. I guess when I was going to a high school in the city it became difficult to get to the city to meet with my high school friends and the summers became rather dull for a while. I guess now, the way things are going, I've gotten back to that, trying to exceed the fun that was had last year with Sarah. I guess I didn't think it was possible to do, considering a lot of my friends have moved away since last summer. Sarah is busy most of the time with her new boyfriend, and Amy is rather lazy and only lies around, but now that I've met Michelle, I feel like it's entirely possible again.

I was down at the beer festival on Saturday with Michelle and her friend who had the weekend to herself. We were just sitting by the water in the park smoking cigarettes when this other lady had begun talking to Michelle. Eventually she decided to sit and stay with us because she and Michelle were both artists. This older lady seemed like she was in rather high spirits and probably a little drunk. As we were all talking, I guess she noticed that Michelle and I were about the same age. Michelle's friend was older but it's only slightly noticeable that she's older than Michelle and I. The older woman was probably about ten years older than Michelle's friend but she was still only in her mid-fifties. Her husband looked a little younger than her, but I don't know how old he was. So in noticing this, the lady asked Michelle if we were dating. "Kind of," Michelle replied.

I felt great, considering the very few times we've talked, Michelle has made it clear that she doesn't date and that it takes her quite a long time before she finds men attractive. She said it takes her two years. Personally, I don't know if I could stick around that long, partially because it really only takes me about three months before I feel like I could fall in love or already be on the way to love. Around the time I turn thirty-three, in October, I'll know how I feel.

When she admitted that we were kind of dating, it was the highlight of my night. I was expecting her to easily say no to the woman but it was swell hearing that little bit of insight into what was truly going on with Michelle. After it got kind of dark, she brought me along with her to her friend's empty house and the three of us smoked marijuana on her friend's king size bed. I don't usually smoke pot anymore—I just had a puff.

Amy was sending me messages all night, asking me when I was coming home. I ignored Amy all night. Michelle's friend drove me home just before two in the morning, and I went home knowing that I was well on my way to topping the summer I had last year with Sarah, almost entirely certain I was going to end things with Amy soon.

I've been excited that my best friend Shawn, the guy who I spent the bulk of my life with until I was about twenty-two is coming to visit me in August. If he was around, I'd probably always have something to do, have more friends, and wouldn't feel alone sometimes because of Sarah's absenteeism that has resulted from being with her new boyfriend. I used to read the same books as Shawn (although he's read a lot more than me), and I used to hang out with all of his ex-girlfriends.

I visited him when he lived in Ottawa and visited him in our hometown and in Ottawa in the summers when I lived in Toronto. I haven't been able to see him since he's been living in Victoria, British Columbia, but we've still been writing together on a blog for three years now and his development as a writer and journalist, even with a degree in journalism, is being forcefully pulled and pushed by my writing gusto at the moment.

I keep a little blue diary that I've been sparingly writing in for about five years now. When he gets here in August, I'm going to have him write in it. That diary is going to be sent to him as a gift once I've finished writing it cover to cover. I've been telling all of my friends, including Sarah and Michelle, about Shawn coming to visit me. It's one of the most exciting things this summer is going to offer and another reason why this summer is turning out to be better than last year's.

I guess the only downside to this summer is that Pastor Derek is leaving. He's moving to Korea. I met him five years ago when I was playing jazz music once a month at a restaurant downtown. The restaurant was having a Christmas party for all the musicians that had been playing there on Friday nights since that fall. Derek was there with his wife and as everyone was saying goodbye to one another, while the restaurant was closing, I struck up a conversation with him.

He had once taught English in Korea and I started talking to him about the oldest board game in the world, which I used to religiously play, and still is kind of well-known in Korea, called baduk. I find it a little odd that our relationship started as a result of our conversations about Korea and baduk, that we started hanging out to play this Korean game, and now after five years, he's leaving to go back to Korea. He came around at a time when I had just moved here and had no friends. He introduced me to countless people and now at the pinnacle of the blossoming of my life (so far) he is leaving. On top of that, his leaving for Korea has made seeing that Korean copy of Hemingway's *The Old Man and the Sea* even more important to me than it should have been.

It has been great to be friends with someone in such a loving and strong marriage because his support has been so valuable to me these past five years, I've grown so much knowing that I've had such a good friend with so much knowledge of relationships. If Shawn was still in my life, he would be my go-to-guy about relationships, the way he always was in the past. He was really the first guy I ever confided in about my feelings for girls.

I used to climb in Shawn's window at three in the morning to wake him up to tell him about Nina and the things that were happening with her, that were keeping me from falling asleep. Nina was the last girl of many, starting with my high school best friend, Stephanie, the first girl I ever slept beside. Shawn showed me a glimpse of tomorrow.

After that weekend with Michelle, the next time I had sex with Amy I thought about Michelle. It drove me crazy that I wasn't in love with Amy, that there was no courting, that it seemed like an agreement to have lots of sex with no discernible relationship bond. Amy had a day off from work last week but Michelle wanted to be with me, as did Sarah. It was another one of those times where fate had provided me with something great no matter what I chose to do with myself. I think that's the view from tomorrow.

I went to be with Sarah, I told her I'd had enough of Amy, and she told me to just break up with her. She explained to me how difficult it was for her to break up with her boyfriend when she was seeing me last fall. I sent Amy the message that I didn't want to go out anymore and Amy said she was surprised. I really hadn't given her any reason to think anything was going badly in our relationship. I think there is a guy for her, he's probably not very active, not very social, likes mundane things like staying in and watching TV and movies, and doesn't need deep conversations to make him feel good.

"I guess that means it is okay for us to go to that concert in August together now, eh?" After I broke up with Amy that was the first thing Sarah said. I told her it was great that it was okay for us to go to the concert and both of us were happy. Then I hugged Sarah, thanked her for her support, and went to see Michelle.

Michelle and I went to the beach and we packed the sand around Michelle's feet to look like she had giant duck feet. It was beautiful out, the scenery was perfect, and I was happy with Michelle, but most importantly, I didn't feel like I was comparing Michelle to Sarah and the strong feelings I had for Sarah. It was just what it was, and it was good.

Most of the time when I see Michelle now, she says she can only see me for a little while but our conversations are so good that we don't even notice six or seven hours passing by as we walk around downtown. We sometimes run into my friends when we are downtown and she buys pizza for herself and I eat it because she's a picky eater. We go sit on the sand at the beach and she tells me about her life and it's interesting. I tell her stories about my life that relate to what she talks about. She laughs lightly at most of my jokes and I carefully ask her to explain what she means when I don't understand her. It's very nice. She's a massage therapist so she has a deep knowledge of the body and science and medicine.

For the past three days, Michelle has driven to New Brunswick visiting her family because her father is dying in the hospital. She has needed a lot of support from me and we have been sending messages to each other a lot. We've also been talking a lot because I've been taking care of her cat while she's been away. She says now that she's going to stay longer because she will have to stay for the funeral in Newfoundland when her dad dies.

It's sad, but Michelle has told me about her need to make more friends, which explains why she took her earphones off and talked to me at the bus station the day we met. But I don't think she expected that I would become as important to her as I have, especially so quickly.

# Chapter Sixteen

*Wednesday, August 12, 2015*

Pastor Derek is in Korea now. He sent me a message telling me he was having kimchi for lunch as I was going to bed yesterday. I was really only going to church because he was my friend. I see very little reason to continue going now that he's gone.

Within the church congregation there was a faction of people who came to services that were not really believers of organized religion, or as the church presents it. John was one of those people, and so was I, if I'm being honest. John believes in some kind of power beyond humanity and admired the work Pastor Derek was doing and believes in the power of love as the ultimate gesture required by humanity to survive. It's easy to admire John's pursuit to convert everyone into lovers.

John also plays piano, sings, writes, recites poetry, and paints. He is in his mid-fifties and has a girlfriend who promotes love and practices all the same artistic activities. John encourages me.

If there was a strong man that anyone could look up to for

advice on anything, and trust, it would be John. He's been rich and he's been poor and prefers being poor. He's somewhat up-to-date about my goings-on with the women in my life and he encourages it as well. He says I seem a lot clearer with my thoughts than I did before. He attributes it to the fact that he says I'm a lot healthier. I, myself, attribute it to the fact that I've been writing so much.

When I was emotionally busted after Nina and I had a falling out and I moved back to my hometown, I was very distraught for a number of years until I started to write my first book. It's a long book that still isn't finished. When I started it, my thoughts were so unclear that it makes most of the book very difficult to read. As I continued to write and the years went by, my writing became clearer. I couldn't finish the book because it became impossible to go back and rewrite what I had written when I started. In some places, I only have a vague idea of what I was trying to communicate.

One line I wrote though, equally as vague as the rest of the book, stood out. "April looked in December, the month following Monday," it said. That was the line that got me into bed with the girl who took my virginity around this time in the summer, about half a year after I had written that line.

Her name was April, the first and last girl named April I ever met. She sat on my lap at a party we were having at the rooming house I lived in, in my hometown, and told me her name. I told her there was a character in the book I was writing that only appeared for one line. I recited the line to her and she acted extremely excited about it and she began telling people at the party. She came back to me when I was alone and started taking off some of her clothes for me. We quickly scurried off to my room. We had sex, but I didn't kiss her. It was then that that line with no real meaning instantly became the most important thing I had ever written.

John has known me for five years now, about as long as I've known Pastor Derek, and he has never seen me with a woman in those years, except since last year. He has seen me with Sarah and Amy and has already seen me with Michelle. For some strange reason, it seems like he's been the only one to have witnessed and been around to talk about the transformation I've had. He describes it to me but I still think the best reason for any kind of apparent transformation is a result of writing, and to a lesser extent, a bit of luck, despite the fact that Sarah started going out with her boyfriend on St. Patrick's Day, which is exactly the same day Valerie stopped talking to me last year.

I had been spending weekends with Michelle but since she is in New Brunswick visiting her sick father, I had nothing to do last Saturday, so I visited John. He's been having relationship troubles with his girlfriend and they had had a sort of temporary break the last time I saw him. This time John was out on his girlfriend's patio playing his keyboards when I stopped by. He seemed delighted to see me. He was upset that this other man had taken his girlfriend out to Toronto to look at music stores and to go for dinner. As John tells it, this other man has been in love with his girlfriend for some time. This made John terribly upset and he wouldn't stop talking about it all night.

I couldn't help but notice where I am with Sarah, that I am that other guy in love with her. I kept repeating that really there is nothing I can do about the situation with Sarah, just as this other guy probably can't either. Our conversation went on through the early evening. The more he said about this guy infiltrating his love life, the more it felt like I was eavesdropping on a conversation had by Sarah's boyfriend about me. Regardless of the fact that John was unhappy, he was alone, and I brought him some necessary company until his girlfriend came back. Just before John's girlfriend came back, Sam sent me a message telling me he was drunk with Shanna by the lake.

I met up with the two of them by the lake. They were wobbling drunkenly towards the carnival that was in town. As soon as I got there, Shanna started insisting that Sarah was supposed to have met her. By the time we reached the carnival, Shanna had called Sarah about five times and left three messages on her answering machine. Sarah finally said she was with her boyfriend. I told Shanna not to tell Sarah I was there. We bought tickets at the booth and Shanna won a stuffed animal by shooting a basketball into a net. We went on the UFO and then on the Ferris wheel. We took a bunch of pictures on the Ferris wheel together.

When we were done with the rides, Sarah confirmed that her boyfriend had left and that she would come meet us downtown to go for beer. She didn't know I was there. It was great because two days before that, I was supposed to go to another underground rock show and meet Sarah's boyfriend, but didn't go because I didn't want to meet him. I thought it would be uncomfortable for me. I was a little skeptical as to when I would see Sarah again. But she rode her longboard downtown, and met us at the convenience store where I was buying a pack of cigarettes.

We couldn't decide which bar to go to. They were all busy because there really aren't a lot of bars to choose from. It's just one small main drag and that's about it. One of the bars wouldn't let Sarah in because she had a longboard and said it was a safety hazard. We finally found the bar we liked. It was extremely busy and we bought a pitcher of beer to share between the four of us.

Shanna seemed on edge all night. Shanna and Sarah talked

for the entire duration of us drinking the first pitcher and Sam and I couldn't hear the two girls talking on the other side of the table because the band was so loud.

We went outside for a cigarette after the first pitcher and Sam and I started talking about women. I told him I really wasn't sure what I was going to do about finding a girlfriend and that I was kind of worried that my chance with Amy might be my last. He told me not to worry. When we came back in we went to the patio at the back of the bar and the four of us sat aligned on one side of two tables that were beside each other. We could all hear each other because the band was quite far away. Sam and I kept talking to each other.

At some point the two girls left us to go out for a cigarette so Sam and I started talking about women again. I guess to get on my good side he mentioned that he had an intuition that I had very strong feelings for Sarah. I guess he wanted to seem like he was interested in what was going on with me but really he was worried about himself. He felt guilty.

"Can I tell you something? You have to promise you won't tell Sarah," he asked me. I told him I wouldn't. Then Sam acted apprehensive about telling me but he finally did. He told me he was cheating on Shanna. Then he added to it by telling me he had had a threesome with Sarah and his girlfriend a long time ago.

"Don't look at me like you're going to kill me," he said. I suppose I did look rather upset so I calmed down a little bit. I don't think I'm going to mention hearing about their threesome to Sarah. I guess he told me all of that because I told him about my sexual experiences that I had with Sarah last fall. It was a little bit of tit for tat and he won. This is one of the reasons why I don't like younger men. They are very competitive.

Shanna and Sarah didn't come back for a while so we joined

them at the front for a cigarette. When we got outside Shanna and Sarah had somehow convinced some guy to take them back to his place and they were trying to get the guy to allow us, their two male friends, to come too. He saw us and quickly changed his mind about having the girls over. As he was deciding, Shanna came over and told us that we were all going to his place and he was going to give us more beer. At the time, it seemed as unlikely to me as it truly was.

The two women started making fun of him because they were upset they couldn't use him for beer and then the guy called Sarah a cunt and some woman on the sidewalk stepped in and slapped the guy telling him not to call a woman a cunt. Then I asked if she would slap me because I liked being slapped. "You look too nice," she replied. The sidewalks were crowded with people that the bars had emptied out onto the strip after closing time. Then the four of us decided it was swell and walked together back home.

As we were walking home, I grabbed Sarah's longboard for a quick ride up and down the street. When I came back, Sarah said: "Let me get on." I moved my feet to the front of the board and she put her arms around my waist and we rode the longboard together to the end of the street. We all lived fairly close to each other. We did until Sam and Shanna broke up a couple days later and Sam moved out of their place. The day after they broke up, Michelle's dad died.

Her cat was very despondent and withdrawn for the first week she was here, but for the past week she's been cute and cuddly and playful with me. I think the pictures of me with the cat and the descriptions about how playful her cat is, have cheered Michelle up a little bit. We've been sending messages a lot back and forth while she's been away. She should be back by the weekend, but Sarah and I will be going to Toronto to see a festival, that for the duration of my relationship with Amy, we weren't really sure we would be able to attend. I'm looking forward to it, but it's kind of sad that it's now the second week of August and we still haven't gone to the beach once.

When I told Michelle about my recent break up she was surprised I had a girlfriend. I told her all of my reasons for breaking up. "And she would never sleep with me," I included. "But that's the best part," Michelle said.

# Chapter Seventeen

*Monday, August 17, 2015*

Last Saturday we went to Toronto at eleven in the morning. Sarah's best friend drove us to the subway station on the northernmost side of Toronto. I wanted to visit some of the old hangouts, but I wasn't sure we were going to get to because Mac DeMarco was performing at a park on the south side of Toronto, a few hundred meters from Lake Ontario. When we got to the subway station agent to buy tokens, he sold us a family pass to give us unlimited trips on the transit all day. As soon as we got that, I knew where to go.

We took the subway downtown, near the University of Toronto campus. I remembered a beer store that was close to the station where we stopped. Sarah had been up drinking at her place until five in the morning the night before, so we stopped at a bar first so she could drink a Caesar. She said it was her hangover cure and it worked every time. The Blue Jays were on a twelve game winning streak and there were couples and middle-aged men watching the game against the Yankees in the bar.

One man sat right next to me yelling as if he was trying to be heard in the upper deck of the stadium. I began rushing Sarah to finish her Caesar.

When we were done at the bar, we went right next-door to the beer store and bought a bunch of beers. Sarah already had brought three beers in her purse. When we left the beer store, I took her to a park off of some of the side streets near Bloor and Spadina. It was a park just behind the Royal Conservatory of Music. When we're home, we go to the park with beers and play guitar and talk and laugh. It was the same except we were right in the middle of downtown Toronto. I remembered that park. I called Nina from there one day before our falling out.

When we were in the park, we took pictures and videos together with our phones. I told Sarah that I didn't think I'd ever have a girlfriend again. She tried to cheer me up for a while. I knew I had to get out of the sad mood that had been gnawing at me.

She told me the worst possible thing she could have, though. I guess she was trying to say that I shouldn't try so hard, I needed to change my routine because I was becoming monotonous, and something would come along. Then she told me about her strategy for meeting her new boyfriend. She said she knew that one day they would be together, and her determination to be with him got her what she wanted. She told me she sat beside him in class one day and he had his phone and she commented on it and told him he should take her number. Another time, she suggested that she didn't want to be alone when her group of friends had to go, so she asked him if he would keep her company. I told her that girls don't fall for me that way. They only do that for attractive men.

Since then I've come to reconsider the notion that I am tomorrow. Her boyfriend is tomorrow. Just then she had perfectly described him as being tomorrow. At best, I am the dew. In the summer, around midnight, on hot days, the grass gets a layer of dew on it. I have no idea what it's from and it's not even noticeable when your heart's full of wine but when you notice it, it's beautiful. I noticed it first when I used to play all night hide-and-seek with the other kids from the neighbourhood. I had forgotten about it for so long. It's the cusp of tomorrow, it lasts longer in the fall, and when the dew starts to become frost, it stays until midway through the next day from September through November, until the snow starts coming.

I remember it the night I was looking for a cigarette and I was bewildered by Shawn's red eyes. That night, Nina appeared to me in my kitchen. I had just eaten some mushrooms with Shawn while playing baduk on a board made of African blackwood. Her smooth brown hair glistened like millions of the little sparkles you see in the snow banks, under the streetlights, in the winter. I wanted to touch it. I wanted to take her light frame and put it on the kitchen counter and press my lips to hers. I leaned in to kiss her. As I got closer she belched defensively in my face.

I ran out the door and walked around the apartment building. Out of exhaustion and frustration, I fell flat onto my face on the dewy grass. My clothes got damp as I lay there. As I lay there, the dew helped me regain my composure. *It's too late tonight, and I need more time, I need another day, I need tomorrow, and judging by your presence, it's bound to come for me.*

"How do you know it won't happen for you?" Sarah asked.

"Because that doesn't happen to me," I stubbornly admitted.

"How do you know?" she insisted.

"Because it won't."

"How do you know?"

"Because it won't!"

She told me I was the most stable person she knows, too. Even that didn't cheer me up. I purposefully let her get off of that topic because I didn't want to beleaguer our time together. We were there to have a good time and I didn't want to ruin it. Besides, I get the feeling she looks up to me and it probably strikes her as odd that things are likely to not work out for me. Or what's more likely is that things work out for her, and she doesn't understand that it doesn't happen for everybody.

But we began taking pictures and videos after that, and she put my long hair (I had been growing it for over a year) in a ponytail for some pictures. She told me it looked good so I left it like that for the rest of the night. I got one video of her rolling down the little hill that was on one side of the park. We spent most of the day there. We could have gone to the festival earlier to see some of the other acts but we really only wanted to see Mac DeMarco. As the afternoon turned into dusk, we put our last two beers into Sarah's large water bottle and made our way back to the subway station. The subway seemed to be closed so we hopped the turnstile, got on a subway car and passed the inconspicuous bottle full of beer between us.

We finally were at the festival and there was a huge crowd in the park. We took more pictures at the festival, we bought beer from some of the festival vendors, and before too long, the sun went down and it was evening. We weren't paying much attention to the concert when we first got there but finally I noticed Mac was on the stage. Sarah went absolutely insane when she saw him. She grabbed my hand and we walked closer to the stage to get a better view. "Back in Toronto again," was the first thing Mac said into the microphone. Then, just as scheduled, Mac and his band began playing their first song at exactly eight-forty.

"Still together!" we shouted at Mac in between songs, in hopes that he would play it, our favourite song. We knew, and sang along to all of the songs he played. Sarah could barely see over the people in front of us and most of the night we held hands walking across the park to find a good view for her as she exclaimed things like: "He's so amazing!" and "I need to see him!" It happened so fast. "We've got one more song for you," Mac eventually had to say to the crowd. Sarah and I then shouted as loud as we could. "Still together!" Mac then began playing the chords to his last song. It was *Still Together*. It's a slow song so Sarah asked me to dance with her.

In the middle of the park, we danced to Mac DeMarco playing our favourite song while shouting the lyrics as loud as we could. "STILL TO-GE-THER!" We sang as loud as we could, holding hands and spinning around and around in a wobbly drunken sway. We probably ruined the last song for some of the people around us but we didn't care. It was only for us. We were meant to be there together. As he finished the song, we saw what time it was. We had just enough time to make it back to the station to catch the last train home. As we were leaving, Mac was saying goodbye to the audience. Luckily, we didn't miss a thing.

As we got on the train, Sarah told me I should come back to drink some more at her place, when we got home. I told her I would. We both fell asleep for most of the ride home. It was just before we pulled into the station back at home that I woke up. There was an announcement: "Last stop, the train is now out of service!" Sarah was still in a deep sleep. I looked at her sleeping before I woke her up. I looked at her legs and I could see her underwear through the spaces between the buttons on her skirt. Many times, Sarah has told me she doesn't like her legs, she says they are too big. For some reason, her legs are the part of her body I desire the most. I grabbed her thigh and shook her leg until she woke up. We got off the train together and I told her I wasn't going to go over to her place and we could share a cab back to Newton Street.

# Chapter Eighteen

*Wednesday, September 2, 2015*

    It was partly because I needed a change and partly because of Amy that I moved into a new place a couple of days ago. I also quit smoking, and went to the hair stylist to get an undercut just like the trendy hipsters are doing these days. Sarah convinced me to change my hair when she put it up into a ponytail while we were at the park in Toronto. I don't know if I'll meet anyone because I'm breaking out of the little routine that I developed, but I got four compliments about my hair, from the women at work. I was noticeably grumpier around Michelle the other day. I think smoking made it easier to keep calm.

    It's the beginning of September now, but the weather is still in the high twenties and low thirties during the day. There's no frost yet. I feel that based on past experience, fall has seemingly been my time of year. It's only been two months that I've known Michelle and it's really too soon to turn that into something more than what it is. It's currently mostly us wasting time together, going for walks, and her telling me about her ex-husband and guys she dated after her marriage broke. I am slightly attracted to her, and we get along well. When she came to pick up her cat the night she came back, she introduced me to one of her sons. She introduced me in a way that made it seem like I was special to her, like she had mentioned me while I wasn't around.

At first, her assertion that it takes her two years to find a guy attractive seemed like it was a way for her to make sure I understood that we were only to be friends, and it still may be just that but her pace and how we are together suggests to me that she isn't really capable of speeding up the progression of any relationship. In the past, before I was able to develop any kind of quick affinity with women, I found that I had a lack of sophistication for reciprocating the tempos that they were dishing out. In conversation, I would jump to things that might concern situations months away and not answer the pertinent questions thoroughly. I think it's different now because my thoughts are clearer and I am able to focus so as to listen and relate to subjects that are in the here and now. It doesn't change that it's going slow and Michelle seems to like it that way.

Sarah got two part-time jobs last week and she hasn't been able to make herself available for more than one short three hour visit to check out my hair, giving me my fifth female compliment for the day. With her, she put the moves on me within the first month of meeting and didn't avoid being alone with me at my place. Although Michelle refuses to come over, the amount of time I spend with her reminds me of the attention I was getting in the beginnings with Sarah. It just seems that there will be no coincidence this time. The fall is not going to be the start of another new intimate relationship. It's too soon, the tempo is too slow, and I really have no reason to think Michelle is even interested in me on that level.

When I was with Shawn almost a month ago, I blatantly told him I truly missed Alaina. I've mentioned Alaina a few times, but didn't really describe the nature of the profound impact that woman had on me. I met her because Shawn dated her in high school. Alaina moved away for her second year of university, and I've seen her once since. I have no idea how to contact her even if I wanted to and if I have any one regret, although I didn't mention this part to Shawn, it's that I shouldn't have stopped seeing Alaina because she never wanted to be more than friends. There's no telling what would have happened in those passing years, twelve years in fact. So, I don't want to end things with Sarah and I don't want things to end with Michelle.

The last time I saw Alaina, I told her it was more difficult for me to see her because I had feelings for her and I thought it was best that I didn't see her anymore. Then I insulted her, saying that her head reminded me of a chicken the way it moved. I don't think she understood, but it really had nothing to do with any of it and I hope she doesn't think about that moment when she remembers me. I went back to my place in Toronto and I never saw her again. It's sad, I wouldn't want that to happen with Sarah and it's a little too early for me to have feelings like that for Michelle. The speed it's going with Michelle, I can't imagine I will ever have strong feelings like that.

Maybe that's a good thing though because everyone always says that relationships come when you aren't looking. For whatever reason, that's what happened with Amy, now that I look back on it. I remember how I felt just before all of that occurred with Amy. I'm not quite sure how to get those feelings back and really harness that feeling so that I'm completely in control of my *relationship destiny* but if I could put it in a Tupperware container and use that place I was in, whenever I wanted to, I would. It was a combination of everything happening with Sarah, and particularly how it seemed like it was drawing to a close but didn't and resolved into a celebration of the fine weather, guitar playing, longboarding and the summer holiday, all at a breakneck speed.

Shawn and I had a couple beers at the Irish pub downtown. We talked about women. My three in the morning, self-imposed interventions had been moved to three in the afternoon this time. I never told him this when he was here but I think it was difficult finding women before he was married. It was kind of a challenge to convert a woman when tomorrow was standing right beside you all the time. We went back to my place after that. I had a half-drank beer and one full beer. I gave Shawn the full one. He wrote in my little blue diary:

*Elliot,*

*Here we are again…*
*Conversationalizing, making time and taking in music, still knowing each other. Ontario is real, and you are real, and even though I am real here seeing you again, a little part of me feels like a ghost,*
*Because…*
*Because…*
*Because the echo of the sounds and thoughts that you and I have together now has a history like rich, old leather, and one day will resonate through us with the cracked and wheezing laughter of us as old men.*
*If you hold down this side of the continent, I'll hold down the*

*other, and I promise you'll always have a safe place to land with me, whether you actually visit, or just vibrate over the telephone,*

*Shawn*

We took a picture, put it on the blog, and that was the first time I've seen him since we became thirty-somethings. I still haven't met his wife. I've talked to him since, so I know he made it back to Victoria, British Columbia.

My room is bigger, the lighting is better, the walls are dark blue and infinitely more vibrant than the dull, drab light brown of my last place. Not only that, but I left my chair at the old place and got a little loveseat from an elderly couple that lives near my parents. My lava lamp stopped working. I take it as a sign. It was always turned on, except when I felt things were going badly with Sarah. I haven't cared to use it as a marker for quite some time. But it gets dark around eight-thirty in the evening now and I tried to turn it on so I wouldn't come home to a dark room when I went out for a walk the night I moved in. I'll have to replace the bulb.

I bought that lava lamp when I was on a date with a woman I met just when I moved into the last place, two years ago. I went on three dates with her, then she stopped answering my messages. For whatever reason, there seemed to be no affinity with her or any other woman back then.

Next week is the start of college again. I look forward to seeing all the people. Sarah won't be there this time, though. I'll probably spend most of the first week there because colleges in September are so vibrant with enthusiastic people. Colleges are a really great place to be in September. I should know, I've been in college for thirteen years now—a combination of past failures, and a more recent drive to be successful in the relaxed pace of part-time college studies made up that time. I'm almost done, and a little concerned that it's going to take me a long time to move on from being in college. Though, I'll have to deal with it when it comes.

Michelle went to college. She mentioned to me that there's a time just after college that one spends having a lot of anxiety because they don't really know what to do.

I think I know what I want to do. I think I want to write every day for three months, describing every detail that happens with some new woman to document perfectly my three months to love phenomenon. I think it would be a little easier to document the happenings with Michelle because she doesn't drink and therefore I wouldn't be incapable of writing because of hangovers. Although, I think drunkenness makes things more interesting most of the time. I have very little faith that sex would have happened in my life without alcohol. Maybe that's a bad thing, but I was always just in for the ride with the other women.

Regardless, if this is how it's done by sober people, I'm curious to find out. I was pretty sober for the most part of my time with Alaina and if it wasn't for Sarah in my life, I'd want Alaina back so bad I'd turn to the bottle to cope. Perhaps sobriety is more rewarding in the end. It was great when I was in grade school. I wonder if it could be as great even though Michelle says she can't run well enough to play hide-and-seek.

# Chapter Nineteen

*Friday, September 11, 2015*

I walked in the rain tonight. It's nice to get out while the rain is still warm. A month from now the temperature will be too cold to walk in the rain. I'd get sick. I remember shortly after my nineteenth birthday Alaina came to my house in the rain. I think she was on a date that night. She brought some guy over to the apartment I lived in with my sister. I suspected that her date wasn't going so well. I'm guessing the young man she was with that night wasn't terrifically excited to come by my place. I've always wondered why she brought him that night. Sarah has never appeared at my place unexpectedly, nor would Michelle. She doesn't know where I live, since I've moved.

Michelle has begun to talk incessantly about her unsatisfying obsession with another guy. She still unfailingly insists on talking about it while I'm with her. As a result, I have very little interest in spending time with her anymore. On top of that, she maintains a profound relationship with her ex-husband. She seems completely incapable of cutting ties with him and moving on to a new life. Her relationship with her ex-husband surely would scare away just about any guy who might develop strong feelings for her, not just me.

Still, when I got paid last, I took Michelle to the vinyl record shop downtown. I told her I wouldn't take long because I was only looking for one thing. I arrived at the record store and located the Leonard Cohen section and it was just my luck that they had what I was looking for. They in fact had two Leonard Cohen albums I was looking for. Now, I have no money. I have five dollars left until next week, I've relapsed into smoking again, and I haven't enough money to pay for another cigarette.

I shouldn't blame my insolvency on Leonard Cohen though. I also had Sarah over for beer and wine. After we drank in my room, I bought a pitcher of expensive beer at the bar. We took a cab home.

Often times, when I come home from the bar, I just lie on my bed and think about getting a phone call from a woman. Coming home from the bar on my own doesn't feel satisfying. In fact, many times I haven't gone out to meet people at bars because I felt as though it was more desperate than fun. I've never met anyone at a bar, except Lella, and still, I never became close with her or spent any time alone with her. She just happened to be there when I had to replace the presence of Nina. I'm not really sure any more if there is any benefit to going out to the bar. It does suit dancing and meeting with male buddies quite well though. But those activities, however, are restricted by my tastes to very short durations.

Yet, I remember, like it was yesterday, the fall that the World Trade Center came down, in New York. I remember Alaina calling me at three in the morning, that fall, after I came home from the bar. She must have called me early in the evening while I was out. She probably wondered where I was and concluded I was out for drinks. I told her it was perfect that she called me at that time but I didn't tell her where I had been. We used to talk on the phone until we were deathly tired in the early hours of the morning. *Grey is what* she called it when we were almost asleep while talking. She said she'd always talk to me when we were *grey*.

It wasn't completely unusual. On a few occasions we would synchronize, over the phone, playing the Leonard Cohen compilation album we both owned. Slowly as the songs passed, the albums would become more out of sync.

Looking back, I get the feeling that nineteen is not the X-rated age that I had hoped it might be. Nonetheless, it is an important age to Canadians and it was an important age to me because of Alaina. Because of Alaina, I fell in love and it's the last love I remember that was healthy. I guess in a sense, I lied to Sarah about having never loved before. However, I never loved anyone before like the way I loved Sarah. I have to admit though, the pain of the love between us, as it fizzled, was much greater than with Alaina. The only thing that eased my pain was the loveless sex that happened after Sarah and I had fizzled.

Most of the songs that Alaina and I loved are on that one album I was looking for with Michelle. I thought it was important to own the album as it was originally produced, since most of it is terrifically important to me. There was one song on the album I found with Michelle that I had never heard before. It has piqued my fancy like it was a secret message, like it had been written the day before I purchased the album. It's called *Winter Lady*. It's about a love that fizzles out in the winter. But what it also hints at is that this winter lady comes back one day when the man no longer has any need for her. You should know I do feel as though Sarah will come back for me one day. You should know it isn't going to be Michelle that relieves my need for Sarah. You should know this is a loveless fall, the kind like when I was a child.

I suppose the thing that makes a loveless fall enjoyable is the lack of feelings of lust. It is one thing to be sexually satisfied, but having feelings of lust on a regular basis is also quite unsettling. I should take up finding male friends this fall. When love comes around again, at least then there will be a friendship to neutralize the oversaturation of lust that has plagued my past loves. I could be wrong, but an overwhelming presence of lust when in love is not beneficial. It makes one clearly unclear.

After Halloween that year, Alaina called me and told me she was going to sleep over on Friday. We spent the evening together in my living room and when bed time came, my lust overwhelmed me. She had no lust. It was just me and I left her there on the couch and headed for my bed. I wished that I had asked her to come to bed with me. She had left her school bag in the hallway outside the kitchen. I woke up in the middle of the night, took her school bag, opened it and pulled out her extra pair of underwear, and stared at it while masturbating. Surely, this is a male dilemma, a nineteen-year-old-male dilemma, an adolescent Elliot dilemma.

I find it very difficult to believe that, between the ages of nineteen and thirty-two, I went from being completely overwhelmed with lust on a regular basis, to almost having no lust for any woman at all. A lot sure changes in those fifteen years.

It takes great strength to overcome lust. In any event, I don't have the strength right now, and I'm hoping it will never again take me nine, or eighteen, or eleven years to ascend with the strength again. The strange thing about how last year, with Sarah and the two sisters, all occurred, is that it felt as though it was women giving me the strength and leading me into ascent.

Since the new beginning of the school year, I've met two male strangers at the smokers' gazebo on campus. I spend a lot of time there on weekdays. "You say really interesting things," one told me. Another guy called me over to talk to him, just outside Tim Horton's, as I was going to meet Sarah the other day. Just as I see the resemblance new women have to the women I've met in the past, these two fellows remind me of the key fellows I've trekked with in the past. It's up to me to show the effort needed to put them in the legend on the map we can create anew. A man cannot compliment a man about his appearance nearly as well as a woman can, but men are fully able to compliment a man on the merits of his intellect and ideas.

His compliment has caused me to realize that this entire time I've had a relationship with writing. Without writing, I've really gained nothing. It is the record of my transformation that makes it more valuable, like a picture adds value to a story. Believe me, I have a topless picture of Amy, and I have a picture of Sarah in a bra sleeping on my bed with her back to the camera. It means nothing without the story. Without the story it's just a sad, pathetic lecher with a camera. Without the story, I wouldn't know what to do with my fall. Without the story, I'd have to withdraw into playing guitar and eating pizza.

# Chapter Twenty

*Friday, October 3, 2015*

    I remember it like it was yesterday. It was a year ago, almost to the day. "I want to kiss you," Sarah said. We had just left our first performance at the college. We finished playing *Lucy in the Sky with Diamonds* and were walking out of the bar when she pulled me into the smokers' gazebo to kiss her. She was wearing a black dress with thin shoulder straps. When she came to my door before we went to perform I just said "Yep," in approval of her attire. Five nights before, we had had our first kiss.

    We broke her thin shoulder straps while she sat astride me in the gazebo. The security guard walked close to us and shouted, "You're on camera!" There's a security camera from across the courtyard in the center of the college. We got up and walked around the building towards the path that leads to my street. We got to an area in the parking lot where there is a little shed on a grassy patch that blocks the view from most directions. Sarah ran ahead, and turned around. "I want you to fuck me," she said. I moved quickly towards her, put my guitar and bag down and we came together again.

"I love your ass," I said. Something amorous happened. She pulled her torn and tattered stockings down and put my fingers in her mouth and I remained silent as the time seemed to move very slowly. Then something more amorous happened. It felt like about four minutes went by. "I don't know what I'm doing... let me taste your tongue again," I said.

We kissed and then we got up, and walked towards the path, bumping into each other like two intertwined threads. "Why does this always happen in the fall?" I shouted. We stopped and looked at each other in a meaningful way and she reached down and touched me. "Yeah, do that!" I said. "You want me to touch your dick?" she asked. She stopped, and we walked through the path, and she was struggling to keep her dress from falling off. I walked a little farther ahead of her. She wasn't there, so I turned back. She stood there with her breasts bare in the cold night air, standing on what is now my driveway.

"I love the way you look at my tits—you make me feel so beautiful," she said. She walked towards me, and we kissed and she got down on her knees on the lawn with her rear end pointed towards me. I knelt down, grabbed her hips with my hands and rocked her back and forth, gently with my pelvis, with our clothes on.

Then we both got up and walked an unusual way towards Tim Horton's. It was unusual because we didn't walk by my old house. I didn't want to take her there. It was too late and she had work early in the morning. We got to Tim Horton's and she bought a sandwich on a croissant.

We talked about our performance. We agreed we played very well. "We butchered Lucy in the Sky with Diamonds," I said.

"We didn't play that one," she corrected me. I argued for a minute, remembering that we did in fact do that number. What was going on while I remembered playing it? "I'll be right back," she said. She left me at the table while she went to the washroom.

"I was just inside you," I said, just as she was about to sit down, coming back from the washroom. "You almost fucked my brains out!" she said. Then her boyfriend called her, she seemed like she didn't want to talk to him, and rudely let him go after a few seconds.

"That was rude," I told her. She looked at me upset, and called him back as she finished her food. Then she got up, went out the back door, we looked at each other intensely and she pointed for me to leave out the front door. I turned away and left. I woke up early in the morning to go back to the secluded part of the parking lot to get my guitar and satchel and walked home to go back to bed.

I remember fragments of being with Amy, and Anna, but nothing quite so vivid. It's raining right now, and it would be too cold to go for a walk, but I'm going to anyway. Tomorrow is my birthday and I just spent the day with Michelle to celebrate because I have to work tomorrow. Michelle gave me one of her paintings as a birthday gift. It's a very small but beautiful painting and it made me very happy to put it on my wall. If I didn't remember Sarah so vividly last fall and miss her company so much, I would probably fall for Michelle. It took me too long to eliminate the feelings I had for Nina. I don't need around what feels like an ancient love for Sarah Benton.

I need to go for a walk tonight. I'm feeling elated because of the beautiful painting I got from Michelle. I asked Sarah to spend some time with me this weekend but she told me she wanted to spend her days off with her boyfriend. I'm not surprised that

Sarah doesn't want to be with me very much anymore. Even last fall I got the feeling that I wasn't cut out for her. I want to focus on whatever possibility there is with Michelle, how wonderful I thought that gift was, and hugging her today. Writing about that time with Sarah a year ago, now, has killed my high, but I can bring it back if I get away in a peaceful walk tonight.

I need to remember sometimes that the pace I need to go is slowly, like the pace of a walk. If my relationships move too fast, I'm going to give them up, and move on to something that is the right pace for me, if that even exists. It's much easier to use touching and kissing to express my thoughts and love when things are moving too fast. Time stops when you love a woman. I've gotten older, although it seems like only a few minutes have passed by. It's still too soon for anything to happen with Michelle, for me.

I was just waiting for the bus with Michelle last week when I felt the distinct desire to ask her out. My heart began to beat faster and I became anxious and my body refused to let me do it. Next week, she's going on a date with a guy she met on the first anniversary of my first kiss with Sarah. This year, on that day, my mother's birthday in fact, I met Sarah at work.

We bought some beer and drank a few in the park. After I left Sarah, in the park, I went to Amy's house and had sex with her. It was one of the better times I've shared with Sarah since the concert in Toronto. I think Sarah was happy when I mentioned that it was the first time I made out with a woman in eighteen years, on that day, exactly a year ago.

While I was with Michelle today, we ran into my parents. It's the first time any one of these recent women have met my parents. My mother seemed to like Michelle. She seemed extremely happy and smiled a lot. Michelle told a story that was delightful and timely. My parents enjoyed it, and I enjoyed how apropos her story was. Then we went to the thrift store and I bought a shirt. We went for a small dinner and I walked Michelle home. When she gave me the painting, I hugged her. It was the first time we hugged. She hugged me when we reached her apartment too.

I also got a hug from my mother and Cadence. Cadence stopped by on his way from Toronto to our hometown. We used to spend a lot of time together in those days when we were roommates. Almost every night we'd be in my room playing guitar or playing video games. He played guitar for me on several occasions until I fell asleep. He knows me very well and he's a social dynamo. When he was here two nights ago, I felt like he could read my mind. He mentioned that he can't fall in love anymore and he was amazed that I still could.

I'm not saying it's impossible but it seems more likely to me that I may never completely fall in love with a woman ever again. Perhaps it was how much time I spent alone while I let my feelings for Nina dwindle naturally, and the randomness of meeting Sarah Benton that allowed this all to happen, but my times with Amy and Michelle are proving to me that Sarah may have been the last hurrah. It's also becoming more reasonable that Michelle's 'two year minimum' may be an appropriate amount of time to get over Sarah and fall in love again. It strikes me though that I haven't seen Nina in ten years now.

Cadence left in the morning, we hugged goodbye and he left for our hometown. There was no special reason why he came but he did make note that it was close to my birthday. He told me one of his very wealthy friends is taking him to see the first Blue Jays playoff game in a private box behind home plate. The two of us agreed that the Blue Jays making the playoffs, for the first time in over twenty years, is probably the best thing to happen this year.

Cadence is a little older than me, much more socially adept, and was one of my best friends when things ended with Nina. His friendship has always been very comforting to me. It was comforting to see him this year as well, immediately after I realized Sarah wasn't going to spend any time with me on my birthday. Cadence came in the timeliest of fashions to see me for the first time in seven years and drank a few beers with me. It was equally comforting when my parents gave me a bonsai tree the next day, while I was still in a hungover state.

After I hugged Michelle and left her, I went to the mall to look for gloves as I always do in the fall. My hands get cold, they are always colder than the rest of my body and I realize I desperately need gloves. Sometime in the summer, I lose track of my old gloves and I end up needing new ones. Most autumns, I go through the routine of looking for gloves all alone at the mall. I usually feel alone because I remember the first fall I spent in Toronto when I looked for gloves with Victoria. I've been alone every year since then. I usually can't afford the gloves they sell at the fancy shops in the mall, but because I have a job now, I bought some thirty-dollar knit ones.

# Chapter Twenty-One

*Monday, October 26, 2015*

I'm not sure why the lava lamp is on. It's been on and off since I replaced the bulb but I've left it on for three weeks now. When I come home for a walk at night I see a dim light in my window. I think now it's just a healthy spirit of light that greets me when I come home. I know now that as the days have grown shorter, the peak of heat has dwindled to only a few hours in the afternoons, my keenness to be outside is leaving me, and my bonsai tree is a bit of nature that I've stolen to accompany my spirit as it is forced to take shelter this time.

The fall has opened my eyes once again. The leaves adorn my neighbourhood's lawns, which now have frost in the mornings. I wondered, at first, why the leaves had fallen in the spring. Summer has passed and it is unmistakably the autumn. For a few days this fall, though, I thought it was spring. It wasn't until I questioned the usual season that brings falling of the leaves that I realized I had been wandering through oblivion this entire summer. I wandered, why?

The good thing about awakening this way is the realization that when you don't know what time it is, it's of no consequence unless you have some place to be. It reminded me of a time before I ever had any feeling for a girl—the awakening time just after the innocence of being a baby, walking and having a thought. Perhaps they weren't the most philosophical thoughts—thoughts like: "all dogs are boys and all cats are girls," and "the living room is for living, and the dining room is for dying."

And now that I'm a grown man, I have to be at my classes, at work and in bed at a decent hour, and on the toilet in a timely fashion. I have to pay bills, and make breakfast, and go for a walk. I have to hug my mom once in a while and I have to water my bonsai, or cut a pepper before it goes bad, but I'd like to think there's someplace else I have to be. I talked to Shawn on the phone last week. He was playing with his two-year-old at the playground near his house until she became restless and stubborn. He then picked her up and carried her home.

I feel a cognitive dissonance with Sarah now. I've not seen Michelle in a month and I feel that Sarah is in love with me. I'm searching and keeping my eye peeled as much as I can for any place for me to be, beyond the tedium of modern day survival. It's the only free trip there is—love, that is. Sarah likes that my room is blue, so I wish I could paint it another colour. The social implications of our relationship have kept us apart as lovers. The age difference makes things awkward and Sarah is extremely social, and consequently prefers to be accompanied by the very handsome.

Yesterday was my father's birthday. I was with Sarah the previous Thursday, Friday, and Saturday. Her presence and gusto for being here with me are inappropriate, while she maintains an affirmation of love for her boyfriend. Either she loves me, or she is just the most socially adept female I've ever met. How else could she keep up her fervour for me? I can appreciate either, but something tells me that believing in her social prowess is my compensation for the cognitive dissonance I feel. The gravity of our love is keeping me from the places I'm hoping to be in my lifetime. Gravity is pretty permanent.

We played music together and drank beer the first and second days we were together. We drank wine the last time. I asked her if she feels that women are more emotional than men. I told her that I don't think I've ever really made a woman emotional before. I guess I wish she would tell me she felt something for me, try to create a little ecology for us to thrive in. When she leaves, I feel wrong for planting my little seeds everywhere. I'm not malicious or derogatory so it's not terribly harmful but I'm also not a bastard, despite not showing up for my father's birthday to make out with Sarah at the end of last October.

I met a girl on one of those online dating sites, and our date didn't go so well. I didn't like her and I don't think she liked me. I think it's a very ugly way of meeting someone. It doesn't feel organic, and very unlikely that there was some kind of happenstance, ethereal arrangement in progress. It feels like a computer spitting out a number that marks your level of neediness to get where you need to be. I'll be honest again, Sarah woke me up last fall and I didn't have to be anywhere but there. I'd stay with her forever if I could.

"Where did you come from anyway? You know what I mean?" I asked Sarah. It got to the point the last time we were together, when we were drinking wine, that I shouted this at her. I suppose she knew what I meant because she didn't really respond. She came from the ether in some kind of happenstance arrangement. "How did you get here? Did you walk through the park?" I corrected myself. I suppose that's what I should have said if I wasn't so elevated that she was there and in good spirits. She stayed for quite a while that day and we slowly polished off nearly two liters of wine together.

She's coming over tomorrow too. I suppose that in my manic state, unable to fall asleep, I feel as though there is a time someplace in my future where Sarah will not matter to me, I will have a record of when she was my ether, and I will puke in my attempt to taste the bit of the hair of the dog that bit me. There is a precedent for this too, when I read Nina's letters. Before she comes, I'm scheduled to help my sister move everything from her old office, in the morning. She has an office right downtown, where all the shops and pubs are.

I should turn off the lava lamp, but I'm not going to. There's frost on the ground now. If I didn't have shoes, it would be too cold to walk the path I go on in the morning, and when I come home at night, there is a little love that shines dimly. I can see it through my window. The frost is beautiful but the light is ugly. Being is not defined by dimension, and balance is sometimes hard to come by and I'm not completely in control of either, so having a little control of my balance and my being, before the destructive sentiment of winter arrives, soothes my spirit.

Also, I love women who can't listen to the Beatles' *Twist and Shout* without causing the record to skip. Sarah did that on Friday. Thus my light shall shine again through the fall. When she left, I smoked pot and lay in my bed in the dim light, paranoid that Amy had syphilis so I masturbated to get rid of it. I looked up the symptoms in the morning. Amy is clear.

# Chapter Twenty-Two

*Friday, November 6, 2015*

 I had stayed up all night and I smoked all of my cigarettes. My sister gave me an advance payment for helping her move in the morning. I bought a pack of cigarettes, a coffee, a butter tart and a muffin and I had just enough left for another coffee with a quarter left over. I helped her move from her office during the day. She took me for lunch at one of the hip restaurants downtown that is very popular. "Lucky you," Sarah said when I told her where I was being treated to lunch.

 After we finished lunch, I walked down the street to get a coffee at Tim Horton's. As I was walking back to the office to finish moving my sister's stuff, an old man who is frequently downtown begging for money asked me if I had any spare change. I told him I didn't but then I remembered I had an extra quarter so I threw it into his hand.

 My sister came to see my new place for the first time when she drove me home. "Your room is really blue," she said. She gave me a fern and a bunch of plates and glasses from her office.

Sarah was sending me messages all day with plans to drink whiskey with me. As soon as my sister left, Sarah arrived.

We spent a little time together and it was sort of uneventful. She probably has become accustomed to me being depressed sometimes. She brought up the topic of women being emotional again, as if she had thought about it in the time passing. When she left, I admired the check my sister gave me for my work. I hadn't cashed it so I was still broke. I ate stale popcorn for supper that night.

In the morning, I cashed the check from my sister and I sent Michelle a message for the first time in a month. We made plans to meet in the evening. She finally had the van her father left her when he passed. I met her son again. He was getting his hair cut when I met up with Michelle. She drove her son home so we could go for dinner alone at a pub near her place. I had a salad and it was unusually good for a little pub like that. Michelle told me it was usually dead in there. That night, for some reason, it was packed to capacity. She mentioned the guy that she has had a crush on for some time. She recently asked him out despite her shy nature. In all honesty, I don't think he really likes her.

I like her son. He's cute, being that he seems to be aloof most of the time. There's some kind of story regarding the coincidental timing of her sons' birthdates. She seems to like pondering coincidences that occur in her life. It's interesting to me. I've twice called her 'Miss Coincidence'. She seems to like it and find it appropriate. She doesn't seem to like her shy nature, and probably wishes that she had a more social personality. I found it difficult to hear her when she was embarrassed and whispering about her private life in the packed pub. She tries to tell me all of the coincidences that have happened to her with this guy she has a crush on. Most of them revolve around things happening when she thinks about him.

I just think she thinks about him a lot, much as I think about Sarah. Even still, there is a man who apparently sends her money on the anniversary of one of her sons' births because of some crazy coincidence that occurred which saved the man's life that night. I don't remember the exact details but it was the clinching factor in giving her the new nickname.

When we left, I forgot my bag in the back of her van. She dropped me off at the bus station and I took the bus home. When I got off the bus, I realized I had forgotten my bag. I sent Michelle a message about my bag and she told me I could get it from her the next day. I went to bed soon after I got home and the next day was Halloween.

I went for a walk in the morning and went to Tim Horton's as I always do. I spent a little time sending Sarah messages during the day. Lately, she has been more responsive to the messages I send her. I went to pick up my bag from Michelle at seven o'clock in the evening. I met her son one more time.

When I got on the bus to go home, that old beggar was sitting in my usual seat and I found a dime on the seat I took, which was directly behind him. Then just before I got off the bus, a guy about my age wearing a wig and long, fake, pink fingernails looked at me to speak. "I didn't put my bag there," he said and he pointed to my bag. He took his bag, which was at his feet and showed it to me. "Hey! Look at that!" he said. He had the exact same bag as me. I was amazed. The next morning, after I went to Tim Horton's, I found another dime on the ground.

I was reminded of the time Sarah told me that you never know how you're going to meet somebody. "You could find a dime and when you're picking it up, see a pair of women's shoes in front of you then look up and hear her say 'hey, that's my dime,'" she explained to me. I thought about it for a minute, and I've decided that if that ever happens, I'm going to tell the woman, "You're a dime." I suppose that might be a nice thing to hear, despite that people don't really call a beautiful woman a *dime* anymore. Regardless, I have a bad habit of running into significant women significantly more than once and in that time she would figure out what I meant.

I went to work the next couple days. Yesterday morning, when I got up before five in the morning for work, I walked through the park over to Tim Horton's for breakfast. As I walked through the park, I saw the winter sky for the first time this fall. I could see Orion through the clear, dark morning sky, just above the horizon. Usually, I see it sometime in late September. It was so beautiful, and it was especially clear and bright. As I walked through the park, I wanted to prolong the time it takes to traverse it because the streetlights make it difficult to see the stars.

When I woke up today, my day off, I walked to Tim Horton's for a coffee and as I was walking back, smoking a cigarette, nearing the path into the park, I started to cross the street. I looked across the street and I noticed a remarkably beautiful woman walking towards the park and I flinched and for a split-second and almost didn't cross the street because I didn't want to walk by the woman. I did walk across the street, though. I had to, otherwise I would have had to walk completely around the block to my house. As I crossed the street, the beautiful young woman walked towards me onto the street. I was listening to music and could see her speaking to me. "I didn't hear you," I said as I took off my earphones. She asked me for a cigarette.

I gave her a cigarette and looked at the colour of her eyes. She has the same golden coloured eyes as Sarah. She's taller and thinner and she wore silver earrings that were long, silver leaves. She told me she was quitting smoking and asked for my lighter.

It was a cheap lighter I bought at the discount store. She told me it was fancy and I corrected her. I felt something deep, when meeting her, like that meeting was only an undulation of what I could see completely. She said thanks and began to inch herself away. "Have a good one," I said, as I began to put my earphones back on.

"Thanks," she replied, and I walked home. I had a class at noon. After class, I spent some time at the smokers' gazebo chatting with the young college students. I don't watch television so when the conversation directs itself onto the topic of recent television shows, I find myself withdrawn. I mentioned to one guy my interest in baduk, the board game which is well known in Asia. He didn't know what it was and I told him there were more potential game play variations than in chess. He seemed fascinated. I left shortly after and went to the gym for a workout and came home and had a salad.

When I went to see my psychiatrist yesterday after work, the nurse told me I wasn't eating enough and I had to start eating better so I decided that I would go to the grocery store tonight, around five o'clock to get some salad, nuts, bananas, soup, and bagels. I left to catch the bus at the college and the benches were all full. I took a seat on the concrete ledge between two of the benches. I sat there for a minute and noticed that the lady to the right of me had nice legs so I had a decent look. As I looked away from her legs, she turned to me. "Are you the guy who gave me a cigarette this morning?" she asked. To my surprise, it was the beautiful woman who left me feeling like there was more to come.

I apologized for not immediately recognizing her. "I should have noticed the earrings," I said. She touched them and was confused as to whether she should treat that as a compliment or not. I tried to add a compliment so she wasn't confused. She was headed on the same bus as me and told me she was headed to work and her name is Jennifer. When we walked onto the bus I told her to talk to me sometime. We live in the same neighbourhood. Until the weather gets bad within the next few weeks, it is entirely possible that I meet her again.

I went to the grocery store, then stopped by Sarah's work to see her. She was on break, so I couldn't find her. I left and got my bananas and whatnot. I didn't get any soup, because it's pay day at the end of the week and I still have a couple of cans left. After I took the bus back, I stopped at the smokers' gazebo where there were a few people that I recognized from the daytime. It had become quite dark by the time I got back. I think I couldn't hold back how happy I was. The people at the gazebo seemed to talk to me a little more than I'm used to. I was in a great mood tonight. In light of my great day, I'm headed out for an epic walk before I go to bed.

# Chapter Twenty-Three

*Tuesday, November 17, 2015*

Sarah and I brought back empty bottles together on the next Monday. She had the day off. She had been cleaning out her room and packing her things for the past few days. I suppose she didn't realize how many liquor and beer bottles were floating around her room. I got almost eight dollars back and she got almost twelve. She bought us a bunch of beer and we went to the park near her house at the end of Newton Street. The weather has been mild this fall. There's been no snow yet. Last fall, at this time, there was already a bit of snow on the ground.

Sarah's boyfriend works during the day, so she leaves me just before her boyfriend picks her up. I feel a little distressed when she leaves me straight into the arms of her boyfriend. They probably go out to dinner together and go to bed together and it's not pleasing for me to think about. When I got home from the park, I asked Amy if she wanted to have a drink with me at my place. She came and we drank an entire bottle of liquor together. She began talking about some of her delusions again after I gave her a slight kiss on the mouth. It seems as though she wanted to continue talking so there would be no awkward silences, and thus started making up stories.

It made it easier for me to shut her up about her fictional life events by kissing her and feeling her body. As we were kissing, I reached between her legs and she spread them slightly for me. I picked her up off the loveseat, and carried her to my bed. We made love there, and I was too drunk to enjoy it physically. Mentally, it satisfied me and took my mind off Sarah and her boyfriend. After we made love, we watched television together in our underwear. She went home at an early hour so she could get to bed to go to work in the morning.

It has been slow at my work and the next day I decided to go look for some boots in some of the less expensive shops close to the mall. The sole had ripped apart from my boot a couple weeks ago. I couldn't find anything in my price range, except for a small shoe store with fancy-looking Italian boots that probably had been stocked there for years. The store owner said she would take what I could pay but the boots must have been sized for dwarves and I couldn't find any boots to fit me.

After I left that shoe store, I went into the record store and looked at the brand new vinyl records they had. I had never seen an Arctic Monkeys record on vinyl before. Sarah and I love them and used to play a few of their songs at the college last year. I looked at more records and then I found a couple of Ramones records that Amy would have loved. We both love the Ramones. I couldn't decide which one I wanted to buy, but I could only afford one. "Do you need help with anything?" the store clerk asked. I couldn't decide. I resolved to just leave without choosing.

I was walking back to the bus stop to go home when I saw the natural foods store and remembered I needed some bananas.

I stopped there, picked up some bananas, oranges, and soup. As I walked back to the bus stop to head home, a woman and two guys were walking towards me. As they got close, the young woman stared at me quite intently. I was prepared to make a casual glance at her but she fully *eyeballed* me.

When they walked by, I noticed one of the three had dropped a ten dollar bill on the ground. A little girl a few steps ahead of me picked it up as she walked toward me.

When I got home I made some Indian Madras for supper. After supper, I took a walk around my neighbourhood. It was only six o'clock but it was dark, and I stopped on one corner and began to send Amy a message. As I was writing her a message to take me back, the same young lady and two guys that I saw drop their ten dollars uptown walked past again. She looked at me as if this was the resolution of her intent. I didn't finish what I was about to write to Amy, and then I kept on walking. That woman looking at me like that made me think it was a mistake.

Sarah will be gone at the end of the month, and it will be difficult to continue to see her and have the same kind of relationship after she moves out to her parents' new mansion in the country.

It snowed through the night, later on in the week. Sarah had been over, and we drank wine together. We took about thirty pictures together, doing funny things, looking dapper. She had a pretty scarf on, and I was wearing some hip dress pants and a handsome grey cardigan. I haven't really mentioned very much that I'm going to miss her when she moves. I hope she assumes that, but the time will come when her absence is truly felt, and when that day comes, I will let her know.

She finally introduced me to her boyfriend when he picked her up from my place. I laughed awkwardly and didn't have anything to say. He acted like he was he was certain of, and proving his point that I had nothing to say to him. When I woke up, there was a thin layer of snow on the ground. It always reminds me of giftwrap covering a gift. The snow didn't stay very long. It had melted completely by mid-day.

Tomorrow night I will be staying at the hospital to do a sleep study test to prove that I don't have a sleep disorder so I can drive again. After I fell asleep at the wheel, I had a lot of difficulty falling asleep. I would wake up abruptly, scared. I found it difficult to actually fall asleep out of fear. Eventually, that fear dissipated and I was able to fall asleep at a decent hour again. It's been so long since I've driven a car, my life has changed so much for the positive, and it seems like the right time to put my accident behind me.

When I was out for my usual walk tonight, I lost one of my thirty dollar knit gloves. When I realized it was gone, I went back on the exact route I had taken, looking for it. Work has been slow, and it's going to be difficult for me to buy a new pair of gloves that are as nice in the next couple weeks. I'm going to ask Sarah to go with me this time when I buy a new pair. The weather hasn't been so bad for mid-November, I've been able to maintain my usual walking routine without terrible interruption from the weather, and I haven't had much need for the gloves yet.

Sarah left more than half of a bottle of wine here when she came over last. I'm going to have a drink of it tonight, by myself. I had a drink with Shawn over the phone a couple days ago. He was getting lubricated to write a bit of his own book. I suppose there is that which to lament, and that which to celebrate, and I feel this very bittersweet moment so well, and so clearly, and so fondly, especially since to feel the bittersweet moments of life is to feel the best of it all. I will drink alone tonight, but not in total darkness.

# Chapter Twenty-Four

*Thursday, November 26, 2015*

A new friendship has developed with my roommate. He is a Venezuelan spiritual guide. He is concerned that I don't love myself and is worried that I am driven by my ego. We went on a walk with our other roommate, a pretty, young blonde gal. Down by the lake, there is a hill that is steep and goes from lake-level to about a hundred meters high. On the edge of the hill there is a park which is surrounded by trees that have been cleared in one area to create a scenic lookout over the lake and the central part of the city. We went there a few nights ago. From the lookout, it's only minutes from the lake. As we were going down the hill to the lake, I realized how beautiful it was. "I'm surprised we never came here before," I said.

The three of us were new as friends, met as roommates from twenty-two Newton Street, and together on a first journey. I was referring to the journeys I have had with Sarah. I was surprised I never went there before, with Sarah. On our way to the lookout, we stopped in the frosty park across from our house and admired the stars. I looked out, with Mateo, for Orion. We could not see it. I had only seen it in the morning, and wasn't sure where it was located at night. Mateo did spot a strange triangle shaped pattern that looked like the mouth of the Pac-man video game character. As we were coming home, there was an area where the trees weren't so high above us, and just above the horizon, Mateo noticed Orion.

When I saw Orion for the first time last fall, I was with one of Vishal's friends. He was getting married. He was having a celebration for becoming engaged to his fiancée with about a dozen of his Indian friends. That guy always called me Matthew when he saw me walking on the street. He could never remember my name and I think he habitually called all white males Matthew. For some reason, when he saw me that night, he asked me to join him at his engagement celebration. We sat on the patio of the bar in late September, and I looked out at the stars so I could point out how the winter sky had arrived as the group was talking about the cold weather. It hasn't become terribly cold yet this year, but it will. It's inevitable every year. Every fall I have to retreat. Every fall everyone retreats. Every fall, love retreats.

In the morning, the day after we went to the lookout, I went to the little convenience store where I used to buy coffee when I was poorer. I've been getting coffee there again. I was walking through the parking lot, on my way to visit my parents, downtown. I found my other glove there. It had a few leaves on it, and had become a little dirty but it was still in good condition and I was happy to have it back. I told my parents that I lost it, retraced my steps, and found it days later. "That's pretty weird," my father said. When I look at Orion, the earth brings me something. The first time, a dime, and then finally the glove I could barely afford to replace.

I suspect though, that it wasn't looking at Orion that brought me some luck. I suspect that it was simply that I had admired the earth, and the universe. The more I say and think that I admire it, and love it, the more it gives me what I admire, or strange coincidences that leave me in more awe than I was before. It started with Sarah, feeling that way. The right woman doesn't make you love her, she makes you love everything. And despite the fact that love wilts and becomes seemingly lifeless during the fall, I still admire that it is right as rain for the autumn to come. Everything about the fall is beautiful. Before there was love, fall was always my favourite time of year, and really, because it is also so sternly adamant about its rightfulness, I love and admire it as much now as when I was young.

When I was seven, my father used to compost scrap foods in the backyard, the pits of peppers, the skins of pineapples, and things like that. By the fall, a patch of small watermelons had grown in the pile of composting foods. While with my sister, and a couple friends from the neighbourhood, we took the watermelons that none of us wanted to eat and smashed them in the driveway. I remember wanting to go inside because my hands were so cold, but I was having so much fun and I couldn't leave. Those were the days when the snowbanks in winter were taller than me.

Sarah makes me feel young like that. I was remembering that watermelon patch the day I found my gloves and I asked Sarah to come play. She brought over a bottle of wine. I had finally resolved to tell her I was going to miss her when she moves away. "It hasn't hit me yet, but I'm going to get there and I'm going to be like, Fuuuuuuuuuuck! I'm going to miss the city and my friends and I don't really know what it's going to be like yet," she said. She went on, and she talked about what was worrying her.

"I'm worried about Black Friday when I have to work like twenty hours all weekend."

I didn't say much, I just gave it some thought for a while then I realized that it was real, she is really going away. "I tell you I'm going to miss you, and you say 'I'm not worried about that, I'm worried about this.' And it makes sense because it's real. You're really moving, and it is what it is," I told her. I got a little teary in front of her that night. She did too. It wasn't all sad though. She told me I make really witty jokes, and that I always looked good in the jeans I was wearing (the jeans I ripped while longboarding.) I told her she still looks sexy and we listened to music and drank wine like we usually do. It wasn't quite what playing meant when I was a child but it's as close as it gets when you're with Sarah—and slightly more fun too.

There was one thing that she said, which has been on my mind since I found out she's moving. "I'm not real," she said to me. "Why would you say that?" I asked in response. She didn't answer me but the thought that maybe the person or thing that brought me out of my furious anxiety, showed me about nature, and became the lover from my song *Mixing Meta-Flowers* (the song that wasn't meta to me at first, but now will be), wasn't real—Sarah, who, to think I drank on the streets with and taught me how to love again, was not real? The possibility to me that all the coincidences that came about as soon as she became a real part of my life, breathed life on what was permanently stuck in a state of autumn wilting and decay, confused me.

Since then, she hasn't mentioned it. I've been thinking of her for her, rather than how she affects me. I think that's the most important thing. I mentioned that I became friends last fall with a guy who writes. He was into all the same authors as me, had a degree in philosophy, and we became friends because I was carrying the novel, *Maggie Cassidy*, by Jack Kerouac. He finished college last spring, and right on the mark of the following fall, this fall, I met a girl who published a book when she was eighteen and now I go for coffees with her weekly and we discuss writing. I told Sarah that I believe this kind of harmony is provided in nature. "I'm sorry I'm not a writer like that. I'm sorry I'm just your drinking buddy," she admitted.

She has no desire to write books or even read them. It's the encouragement, and lack of competition that made our bond strong. No other woman in my life has ever encouraged me so much. I think even though I have a few years on her in age, when she thinks of people she loves, it's not about herself but about the other person.

I felt no melancholy when she left, that last moment we were together drinking in the park. As we sat there finishing our beers, she began describing a feeling we both loved. The feeling was bittersweet but she was calling it melancholy.

"That's not melancholy, that's, bittersweet," I said. She says it's not the bittersweet that I love. "It's something not really bitter, and not quite sweet, like almost painful but sweet in its infallible truth because it exists like it had been told in a story or a song—it feels disconnected from reality," she explained.

"You're right! There should be a word for that," I said, as we drank our last beer together at the park. She called it *plum*. I had love in the plum moment because I know that it's her change to encounter. I'm just her drinking buddy. It got dark and cold and she left.

I know she's real, but I've learned from her that we are one—as if she is not real, and I am learning from an imaginary projection of what I desire to be. In my little blue diary, the first night we drank together, she wrote, "our hearts beat as one." I suppose in some magnificent view of the giant jigsaw puzzle she sees, by saying she's not real, this is actually what she means. One thing's for sure, though. I've never felt an understanding before, like this. Her nod and tip of the cap to me is thankfully accepted.

# Chapter Twenty-Five

*Tuesday, December 1, 2015*

    Today is the first of December, the month following Monday. It's been a long time since this has happened. It's been six years to be exact. I started my little blue diary six years ago, when I finally met a woman, and then I met another. When I first wrote about April, the character that appeared in my book for only one line, I didn't think much about it, but for the time between writing it, actually meeting April, and now, I've thought about that line so much. It has come to have a deep secret meaning to me. I know that the warmth of April looks to be relieving.
    When I was ten years old, I came across a little blue notebook, packed away in one of my parents' mostly unused dressers. It was about a quarter full of neatly written journal entries. I couldn't tell if the writing was by my father or my mother because both of them had different handwriting by the time I found it. It was written around the time I was born and the stories continued into the first winter following my birth. The entries had stories about a happy couple, what they were doing, the weather that

influenced them, and it was so beautifully written that it was the first bit of writing that really opened my eyes.

Shortly after I found it, I took it and ripped out all of the pages that were written in that book and made it my own. I used the remaining pages with a few friends to pass notes to one another at school. We invented a code system for letters so that outsiders of the notebook-gang wouldn't be able to read the words that had been coded.

In the morning, some of my friends from another class would have the book, and write something until the French teacher came to their class. During the French class, my friends would leave the notebook on the teacher's cart before she left and came directly to my classroom for my French class. I would then pick up the book, decode what had been written, write an entry, and give it back to my friends at recess or later on in the day. We kept up the routine for a few weeks, but never wrote enough to fill the remaining pages of the notebook.

That's the other reason why I started my little blue diary six years ago. As I grew up, I cared very little for the adolescent scribblings I had started and desired to see the beautiful writings that I had once discarded. I thought that someday I might have something genuine to write about. In that way, I could have them back, as meaningful as the pages that I had torn. Because it was December, the month following Monday, the stitch in time that had become divine in my mind, surely something divine would take place.

Nothing happened. Meeting those two women, one after another and seeing them successively leave me was nothing more than a sign. I continued to write as the years passed. I was lonely but I had a purpose. I waited for my secret stitch in time to come again. I gave up on my diary at times, times when there wasn't anything of consequence to write about.

I waited for the next time December would start the day after Monday. Finally, it's arrived and Sarah did not sleep at her place on Newton Street last night. Today she woke up for the first time at her new place, out in the country. It is doubtful that I will see her much anymore. And our relationship will gradually decline into the dust of a memory of something that once was beautiful. I sort of said goodbye and we left on good terms. Her cup is still on my table. She left it here.

I don't feel as though it's a sign that she's gone. I feel as though I did something I had to do. In secret, I will wait the next five years until my secret time comes again and I will fill the remaining pages of my little blue diary and hope that one day my story, too, makes it through the fall. If anything out-of-the-ordinary happens this December, I will make the suitable, subsequent additions. As for now, the meantime, the livid moments of the arrival of this hallowed day—perhaps hallowed month—I will polish one off, polish one off, and polish one off.

Other Books By Michael Whone:

*There Is A Light That Never Goes Out (Bolero Bird/2018)*

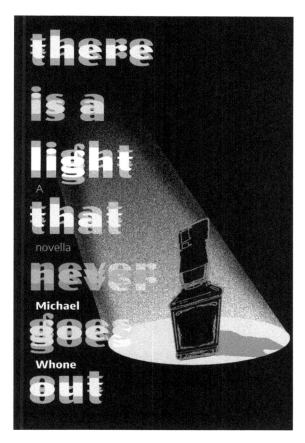

www.michaelwhone.com
www.bolerobird.ca

Printed in the USA
CPSIA information can be obtained
at www.ICGtesting.com
LVHW041530271023
762201LV00014B/1792